Summer Without Mum

Bernadette Leach

Attic Press
Dublin

First Published in Ireland in 1993 by
Attic Press
4 Upper Mount Street
Dublin 2

British Library Cataloguing in Publication Data
Leach, Bernadette
  Summer Without Mum — (Bright Sparks Series)
  I. Title II. Series
823.914 [J]

ISBN 1-855940-744

This book is published with the assistance of The Arts Council/An Chomhairle Ealaíon.

Cover Design: Angela Clarke
Origination: Attic Press
Printing: Guernsey Press Ltd.

<u>Dedication</u>

For Auntie Norah with love and gratitude

BERNADETTE LEACH has lived in Cork since 1983 with her husband and five children. She is also the author of *I'm a Vegetarian* (Attic Press, 1992).

Acknowledgements

I love writing, but it takes time. So, thank you Mick, Paul, Toss, Greg Em and Edward for the chaos, the cups of coffee and the laughter. I'm so glad you're not gourmets but I will rediscover the cooker under the dust!

Thank you Attic Press, I appreciate this second opportunity. To you all, a giant hug.

One

My mother is teaching my brother Ed to drive. She's forty something and he's almost nineteen. If all their mood changes are anything to go by, wisdom definitely doesn't come with age. The driving lessons happen after school. Luckily Ed and I go to different schools. I don't think that I could handle actually being there, in the car, as they wage war. Because that's what it is. On their return the air goes blue and their faces take on an interesting shade of puce. If I'm unlucky I will be sitting in the kitchen, trying to gather my thoughts before gathering my books; exams start in exactly five days time. And one or other of them will come bashing through, red-faced, furious. Whoever has the car keys is the winner. They have become my very own personalised gladiators. Anyone who thinks that well preserved, middle-aged parents are not affected by what they see on television has not witnessed the aftermath of one of Mum's and Ed's driving sessions. Sad!

'If you would listen. When I say brake I do not mean accelerate.' That will be Mum, smashing her house keys onto the work surface, scattering my stash of bottles and glass jars waiting to be taken to the bottle bank. She will freeze me with a look just because I'm there.

'Cup of tea, Mum?' I try. It's a peace offering. Knowing what the battle is about should give me a head start on some kind of treaty. Treaties are in my mind right now; history is my first exam.

'You panic! I saw the van/the bus/ the train ... There was loads of room.' That will be Ed. Opening the fridge and gulping milk straight from the carton once he's sure that Mum is watching, and seething; then he will hand her back the car keys victoriously. Crazy.

It's been going on for weeks. Already I'm a nervous wreck and this is before I've experienced Ed's driving skills. He maintains that all his friends have been on four wheels for years. It's probably true. In Ireland quite a few of the kids he knows live on farms and so have been helping out with tractors and trucks since their feet could touch the pedals. We've only been here for a year, and in England, on the whole, you don't get the feel of the wheel until your seventeenth birthday. Ed didn't have that normal seventeenth or eighteenth birthday. Dad died before the first and he was only settling in here for the second.

'I should have taken up joy riding when I was ten,' he announces miserably, dropping onto my bed and scattering my cat who was peaceful until a few seconds ago.

'You should get proper lessons,' I reply, picking up the angry fur ball and giving him a gentle push outside my bedroom door.

'With what? Ice lolly sticks? I possess ninety-eight pence. Great. Some driving instructor is going to give me ten free hours, I suppose.'

I need to revise; so does Ed. The teachers are calling the events of five days ahead 'tests'. What kind of word is test? These are examinations. One and a half hours of silence is a test of endurance, but it is my lack of knowledge which is about to be examined.

'Get a job,' I suggest. Ed curls his lip. Sorting through my books is giving me a pain in my chest. We have nine subjects. *Nine*! How can I remember one without forgetting the rest? Ed is pondering, his big feet dangling over the end of my bed. He should be working. So should I.

'She's impossible. You'd think I was going at a hundred miles an hour the way *she* carries on.' *She* is Mum. I think she's remarkably brave, or remarkably stupid. I wouldn't sit beside my brother, who has taken to practising racing gear changes with the salt and pepper grinders while waiting for the kettle to boil or the toast to pop up.

'Maybe you're right though.' Good, he's going. I love Ed dearly but he is by nature obsessional. A few months ago it was drumming, morning noon and night. It was as if he was sending out some vital message on assorted tins, boxes, table tops; all very tribal but it made my head hurt. The drum kit is over at a friend's house and that is exactly where it is going to stay. For once mother's brain is working in tune with mine. I almost kissed her when she said, 'No drums, Edward. No argument, no drums.'

Then it was fantasy games. Damien Kelleher and his brother Toby are keepers of the drum kit and other assorted noisy musical instruments. They are also into computers. Damien masterminds the programme making and Toby and Ed supply impossible worlds with diabolical monsters to fill the bytes. And now it's the car.

The phone's ringing. Someone is bound to answer it ... The phone is still ringing. That usually means that Mum is sulking and Ed has gone out. I need to work, I need to work, I need to ... If I say it often enough as I leap down the stairs it might sink in. Probably for all nine papers I will write my name and 'I need to work' a million times on the page. Then I will be carted off somewhere nice and quiet and left in peace.

'Hullo.'

It's Trass.

'Course I will. It might make some of the dates stick in my thick skull.'

Trass, Thérèse McDermot, the first person I really talked to when I started school here. I would hate to do that, start all over again. New people terrify me. She wants to go over history notes. That's good. Firstly it gets me out; the atmosphere in this house is verging on black hole density. Secondly I want to see what she's up to in her house. She's only just moved in.

'I'm going out for a couple of hours, Mum. Over to Trass's.'

I yell this into the silent space between the hall and where Mum is probably hiding – her study. She's busy at the moment, sorting out courses for next year, marking papers. She's a teacher. She prefers to be called a lecturer; that's why I call her a teacher. But to think that I lived with her for thirteen years before realising that she could do a job, earn money and need a study. It's a funny old life!

Trass's place is a good ten minutes walk away. We live in the city. If you live in London, Manhattan or Dublin you will think I'm joking. I thought Mum was joking when she called Cork a city. But I've grown very fond of it over the year. I should look like a bean pole with all the walking that I do. All my friends live close by and I always walk to get to them. But I do not look like a bean pole. I think that there must be a hippo or elephant line to our family. Some distant relative with a trunk and forty inch thighs has finally surfaced in me.

'Can I join you?'

It's Clara, popping out as I pass her house. She lives fairly near me and we're in the same class at school for most subjects. She looks about as cheerful as a butterfly that's waiting to be pressed in a book. This is not her usual style. She has to be one of the most positive people I have ever met. Clara had leukaemia and went through – in fact, is still going through – various treatments. I get annoyed with myself when I have a cough or a cold but she's had to put up with a whole lot more than that.

'Well, if you fancy boring yourself to tears you could always come and check out dates with Trass and me.'

'Save me! Mother has just been going on and on about how little time I spend in my room studying; how she's going to invest in a switch that regulates how often the TV is used ...'

Clara catalogues her woes. At least I can have a moan in peace at home to Ed. Clara's an only child, so she catches all the attention, good and bad.

'Where's she going now?' I want to know. Mrs Farrell, Clara's mum, is driving past us, looking grim and clocking up nought to sixty in about ten seconds. I know about these things – Ed also buys car magazines.

'Who knows.' Clara sighs. I join in. It's a communal 'what can we do with mothers' sighing session.

'I need to work, I need to work ...'

'Pardon?'

'Don't worry, Clara. I'm just cracking up under the pressure.' In two weeks it will all be over. There is hope after May the twenty-third. On June the second the summer holidays begin. I don't think I'll last that long.

Two

The house has turned into a furnace. Even with all the doors and windows open it's like sitting on top of the equator. Why don't examiners give us exams in February? That's what I want to know. In February it's wet, windy, miserable and ideal for staying inside. Hanging around learning about volcanoes and plate-lines and all the other stuff that is rattling around inside my head would be a lot easier in February. But oh no! That would be too simple. I keep looking at my count-down chart above my desk. I've marked off the days in bright pink and glaring green. Eight more and it's all over.

I can't study. It's too hot. I can't have a shower because it's broken. I daren't eat any more or I'll explode. I think I'll make a milkshake. No, I won't. Move over, cat. Why does he always sleep on my pillow? And how do animals survive the summer — all that fur! What I want to do is stop. I need to let my poor over-used grey matter have a break, a long break. I'm dreading the results. There ought to be a health warning attached to this time of the year: Studying seriously damages your mind.

'Vanessa. Vanessa.'

Ah! That is mum and by the sound of it she has slipped into her Mother Superior mode. She can be quite normal one minute and the next you would think that she was auditioning for the Royal Shakespeare Company.

'Coming, Mum.'

10

What have I done now? I brought my dirty clothes down, I unstacked the dishwasher, I fed the feline ... And anything I thought I knew about granite, sandstone, limestone and marble has just slipped out of my brain and flopped into the garden.

'Hullo, Ness.'

It's Mr Fleming. He works with Mum but he also helps us out by mending things, electrical things, which seem to spend their lives breaking down. Dad used to do it. Ed tries, but he seems better at blowing things up than putting them back together again. Not very practical, my brother.

'Is the shower okay now?' I ask.

'Grand. Nothing more than a loose connection. How are the exams going?'

For an old guy he's nice-looking. I wonder why he doesn't ask Mum out?

'Not bad. Well, not good either.'

'I know,' he says sympathetically. 'It's a lot of learning but you'll be fine.'

'I wish. Do you think during the holidays you could show me what you mean by a loose connection? I'd love to be able to fix things.'

'No problem, I'll bring along ...'

'Vanessa!' Mum interrupts and cuts us both off mid-sentence.

No wonder he doesn't ask her out. She sounds like a Lady Macbeth/Boadicea combination. Scarey!

'We need an intercom,' I say cheerily as I walk into the kitchen.

'Where is Edward?'

How am I meant to know where he is? I was in my room having a breakdown over geography. Why didn't she bawl up the stairs and yell 'Ed!' That way she could

11

economise on oxygen. 'Vanessa!' is a lot more effort.

'Well?'

'I don't know, Mum.'

Why does she do that? Ask me instead of him. He's probably gone out, or he's sitting in the freezer chilling his toes. I think I prefer Cork dripping with rain. It's too hot to even think. Anyway, surely Mum has noticed how unhappy he is. Being dropped back a year has left him totally depressed. The more Mum tells him how lucky he is to have this wonderful opportunity of being educated here, the more down he becomes. He's dangerously close to walking away from the Leaving and straight on to the nearest fishing boat. I'll try explaining it again.

'He's finding things very hard. He's bogged down.'

I shouldn't have said 'bogged'. Teacher/mother did not approve. But he is, and he's sinking.

'Vanessa, were he in his room working, he might find life a little easier, but as it is I have just received a telephone call from his form tutor. So far, Edward has missed three tests.'

Oops!

'Now, have you any idea where I might contact him?'

Parents shouldn't have to suddenly contact their kids. If she weren't so busy being busy, she'd see that Ed hates doing honours Maths, Physics and Chemistry. He's out of his depth. Just because Dad was good at the sciences doesn't mean that Ed is. But he *was* good at them in England. It's that he's doing other subjects as well here. Doesn't Mum remember anything about what things were like before?

'You could try ringing Tina.' I feel like a traitor. Tina and Ed have been going out for a few weeks. I like her, but Ed bothers me. I know he's got another year before his final exams but at the rate he's going he isn't going to make it.

'And do you have her number?'

Mum's at it again. It's as if she grows by about two feet. Then her words become precise and icy. Her angry face is like a mask. It's just as well she's stopped smoking. When she's annoyed she gets lots of lines around her mouth. I shake my head. I don't even know Tina's address.

'Stay here. If he returns, inform him that despite my having to teach a class at eight I will miss it to discuss this new stupidity.'

And with that she's gone. What a performer! Since Dad died Mum has tried being either amazingly soft or terrifyingly strict. She's unbalanced. So am I. I can't find my Italian grammar tape. Ed's probably recorded the Beastie Boys over it. Great. Edward Carter, you are in trouble, big trouble. On the bright side, at least tonight I can have a shower.

Three

I hate discussing my private life with anyone. I don't mind listening when other people have problems and I never, ever repeat what they tell me. But when it comes to me, I like to work it out for myself. Right now, living at home is desperate. I can't believe other families are like ours. Mum is so caught up being hurt about Ed's wanting to leave school, this instant, that she has become completely unapproachable. She looks ill. Even though two-thirds of the time I don't want to be in the same room as her, I don't want anything serious to happen to her either. It isn't as if I don't have good friends. I do. Trass and Clara are brilliant, Damien keeps telling me to cheer up and Catherine who's also part of our group at school tried to talk to me yesterday. She thought I was miserable about failing commerce. I was, but that wasn't the real reason. Being Vanessa Carter, stuck in the middle of daily bickering and endless grumpiness, does not qualify me for 'smile of the week' prize.

I ran out of luminous marker before the end of my exam count-down. Remembering to put tops back on things ought to be a New Year's resolution. But seeing as it isn't the new year and it is almost the end of term, I won't add any more pressure to my already stressed-out existence. It's June the first and only nine months ago I walked through the huge front door of the City Community School, looked ahead and panicked. This place continues to be an architectural mystery. Seriously, the outside has nothing to do with the inside. Once you've got used to the shadowy light, there aren't any windows in the main hallway. All you can see are corridors and what the teachers call modules. A module is a little plastic bubble blob, big enough to house the teacher, or headmaster, or whoever happens to be dealing with you on the day. More than two of you in there, and you'd suffocate. I always pray that my breath doesn't smell and that I've used a really strong deodorant. Bubble-trapped, every small imperfection becomes obvious. As soon as I know that I have to go into one the first thing I do is breathe onto the palm of my hand. Do not under any circumstances drink coffee before climbing into this trap. Coffee can leave you seriously smelly.

The headmaster is okay. When I first arrived he made a point of getting to know me. I was a bit pathetic back then. I can be a bit pathetic now, but I hope I've improved. It was kind of him though, and I do appreciate it, but now it is beginning to be a nuisance. Quite often he will stop me as I am going from class to class. He will want to check if things are 'running smoothly'. I wish he would do it surreptitiously, like when I'm dashing to the toilet and everyone else is ensconced, peacefully absorbed and unaware that I am consorting with the enemy. I hate favouritism. Everyone hates a pet, and I could be in danger of being seen as a special case.

'Vanessa, Vanessa Carter.'

I knew it. He's seen me. I was just about to duck outside with Damien, Clara, Trass, Catherine, Patrice and Enda, when ...

'A quick word, please.'

He sounds abrupt. That's his out of office voice. Once inside he's thoughtful and interested.

15

'So, the first year is almost over,' he begins. Terror, he has a list of results on his desk. My 'I must work' mantra is about to be proved a complete waste of time.

'You have done extremely well.'

I wish he wasn't saying all this. I'd rather be told in class, along with the others.

'Commerce was a little disappointing and everything but Italian in the fifties and sixties.'

Oh God! Failure. I was sure there was an A in there somewhere.

'And next year the Junior Certificate.'

Torture me! I know what next June has on offer.

In Ireland all the secondary schools close down in June, which is good for me right now. But they stay open for the poor unfortunates who are doing their Junior or Leaving Certificate. In England, school doesn't finish until the end of July. Whether you are doing exams or not, you slog it through. That's why I want to escape, outside. Clara's parents are taking her to Belgium for a fortnight. Catherine is going to the Gaeltacht. They all speak Irish there, imagine that. I don't know how anyone speaks Irish. I sometimes listen in when they're learning it in class. It sounds like a cross between Japanese, Martian and German. Catherine loves it. She says that she's going to be a primary school teacher, so she has to be good at it. I don't know what I want to be, but I definitely don't want to teach. Look at my mother.

Today is our last full day together. I don't want to miss a moment. We have plans, ideas, and I am a part of them.

'So, what does the summer have on offer?' he's asking. There's a clock above his head. We only have twenty minutes left. Break is almost over.

'We're staying around. Ed, my brother, might be going abroad.'

I can't tell him that Mum and Ed are rowing mightily over that as well as everything else. He would think that I'm crying for help or Childline or something. Ed wants to go away. He told me this morning that an undiscovered planet wouldn't be far enough away. Things are not good.

'Mum and me, I mean I, we're touring Kerry and places.' I sound breathy and anxious and false. Does he know?

'Relax. You've earned it. And congratulations on the A in Italian.'

I got an A. I possess for the first time in my life an A. It's a miracle! I can't believe it.

As I say goodbye and happy holiday to the head, only one thing is buzzing through my brain. I did it. I did it. I didn't want to do it, learn Italian that is. I thought it was a stupid idea, and it wasn't mine. It was Mum's. She and Dad had a second honeymoon in Rome and Venice; the end result of the holiday was me. When Mum explained why she thought it would be a good plan for me to study a language while the others were doing Irish I just felt uncomfortable. I mean, you don't want to *know* things about your parents' past experiences. I don't. But all that business of missing tapes, ordering books which didn't arrive and half listening-in while the others were doing Irish, wearing headphones which made me look like the missing link — it's been sort of worth it.

Four

Making the sign of the cross, the priest leaves the altar. End of term Mass for the examinees is over. I feel flat. Scuttling round my head are the words the priest said in his talk. It wasn't a sermon. He's a chatty new young priest. I almost don't mind listening to him.

'It's on your doorstep, poverty, disillusionment. So, as you lie on the beaches of Portugal and Greece, or watch Fungie, the dolphin in Dingle; as you sample French cuisine and travel on aeroplanes and ships — keep in mind your privilege, your good fortune.'

Guilt. I feel guilty. I don't want to feel that way. I thought that I would want to race out of the church ripping off my uniform as I went. I imagined everything differently.

'He could take the word fun out of fair,' Enda says, interrupting my thinking.

'I suppose,' I answer. But he has a point.

Cork in the sunshine is busy and beautiful. There's lots of action as we all drift onto the street. But I keep seeing things I'd rather ignore. I don't want to see the old lady walking ahead of me with bandages on her legs and a push-along basket. I hate all the rubbish that's gathering along the side of the pavement. People here are bad about litter. I once said it in class and nearly lost a few friends. But it's true. I wish my brain could select good bits only.

'Do not, I repeat not, go serious on me.' Damien, hoisting my sack onto his shoulder, gives me a gentle push.

18

'Smile. That's better. Now, we're having a session at my house tonight. Ed says that he's coming along. What about you?'

Cork has some really expensive clothes shops. In Colchester, where I used to live, I didn't seem to notice price tags. Now I do. I want to be rich. I mean, I don't want to be poor.

'Ness. Would you please, for the love of heaven, stop looking as if you have the weight of the world on your shoulders. Mum is cooking up all sorts of goodies. Well?'

Damien Kelleher's face should be made of rubber. His eyebrows go up and down independently. His eyes crinkle and smile. He has a lovely deep voice and a gentle accent. I like the accent. I'm quite tall but he's that tiny bit bigger. I don't mind walking beside him. In fact, I love walking beside him. I used to wonder about 'fancying' someone. Fancying is a crude word. I like Damien so much. I have some great friends here.

'Probably,' I say.

'What sort of answer is that? Ophelia is out stealing eggs from the free range chickens up the road. Having a politically correct vegetarian come to tea involves a lot of personal sacrifice. Toby is squeezing oranges, just for you. Dad is ...'

The Kellehers. How can I describe the Kellehers? There's Jo and Marc, Damien's mother and father. Damien is the eldest, then there's Toby, Ophelia, Sophie, Darragh, Hugh, Cassie and Chris the twins, and the baby, Tomas. They are an impossible collection. Walking into their crazy house makes *Alice in Wonderland* seem normal. I still get a sort of thrilling shock when I'm there. The only blight is Enda. Jo's niece Enda, who lives with them some of the time.

'I'll come.' I didn't need persuading, but it was nice.

Back at our house everything is quiet and orderly. Walking into the kitchen I notice a big bowl of fruit on the table. That wouldn't last two seconds at Damien's. Jo is forever hiding things like crisps and chocolate biscuits. Toby and Damien go on night raids, apparently, and the first thing they attack are school lunch extras!

Mum's out and Ed is scheming somewhere. He almost got thrown out of school for missing exams. But he's being given another chance, if he goes back in September ready to settle down. As I throw my school bag to the back of the wardrobe I suddenly wish that we were doing something exciting this summer. Ed's organised. He and four friends are going to work in Germany. Mum blames me, not in so many words, but she did say that hare-brained jaunts involving trekking several hundred miles to earn a few shillings did not seem worth his while. I chipped in about how he needed cash for proper driving lessons and she suggested, terribly politely, that he would be better advised to study for his future. I know what she means, so does Ed, but all her nagging is having the opposite effect, plus Ed says that he's suffocating as a result of all the arguing. Give him a break, Mum!

Clara and Catherine are going away on Sunday. And Trass also has plans. Her grandfather is taking her and her Mum to Galway. Trass is incredible. She's a traveller. Her grandfather, old as he is, refuses to settle, but Trass and her mother are staying here for a while. My mother, Jo and Trass's Mum, Marie McDermot, are all friends; it was because of their efforts, plus a bit of push from Councillor Coyne whom Jo knows, that a local housing project has got going. Impressive! Seeing them together is a kind of comedy act. Mum is tall, slim, elegant, 'well-turned out' as my grandmother used to say. Jo is tiny, dark-haired and bubbly. Marie is in between, but a bit thin. She has beautiful skin — it's tawny — and her eyes are almost black. She looks Spanish. Trass has inherited her looks despite having a father who wasn't a gypsy. He's gone. So's my Dad. Trass and I feel like sisters.

Anyway, Trass is in a house now. There are six tiny terraced houses behind the university, where Mum works. Two of them are already occupied. There's Trass in one and the Phelans in the other, Paudie and his wife Cáit and their three children. Damien's father has helped out with a lot of electrical repairs. Some of the people he works with have been doing bits of rebuilding. None of it has been easy because not everyone wants to share their road with travellers. They're sometimes called tinkers or, much worse, knackers.

I had a mammoth fight with Enda when she called Trass a knacker. It was ages ago, but I haven't forgotten. I lost my cool and called Enda every offensive name I knew at the time. Then I sobbed for hours because I didn't know how to make my point about giving everyone a chance. I hate labels, things like, Ness, English, Trass a traveller, Damien oldest of nine. Even though they're true they seem to be saying something else. But I wasn't able to change Enda's attitude and already there are problems with the long-term residents near Trass's place. Petitions have been signed and letters sent to the local papers about property prices falling when 'undesirables' move in. I tried writing an essay on the problem for a school assignment. Trass isn't in my class, so she didn't have to know. But I wanted to get the feel, from my own age group, of what the real scene is. I shouldn't have bothered. Despite all the work I put into it, it still ended up preachy and one-sided. I was almost eaten alive by one or two strenuous boys of the anti-traveller brigade. I suppose it is all going to take time. I wonder if I could be as brave as Trass, her Mum and the Phelans. Because they're the ones who are having to cope with all the abuse and nasty looks.

Being on my own in the house is good. It gives me time to think. I don't want it for too long, but for a little while it's great. Puss is stretched out on my window sill, in the sunshine.

'You could always go outside, cat,' I suggest.

No, that would be too easy. My cat has to be the laziest and most impossible-to-train creature that ever existed. I found him, half dead and hiding in bushes in the garden. Back then, I don't think he had ever seen the inside of a house. Now he refuses to move from the comfort of my bedroom. Occasionally he goes for a night-time frolic and I worry until he's safely indoors again. He's good at catching rats and pigeons when he remembers to wake up! I'm going to sit outside for a while. I can't believe it. I am on holiday. And I feel ... low.

Five

Today the sun is shining, the sky is blue, the birds are singing. This is the beginning of a new life. I could write poetry about today. I might even pen a song that will rap its way straight to number one. It is *holiday time*. Day five and the euphoria hasn't left me. It's the no-more-alarm, no-more-forgetting-my-homework, no-more-lousy-school-uniform feeling. Essays can hang themselves. Verbs can go into permanent decline. Maths? I don't ever want to think of another formula for the rest of my days. Today I am going to play loud music, so loud that Mrs Fogarty who runs the corner shop is going to think we're having a rock concert in the back garden.

This summer I am going to get brown. I am going to grow my hair, again. I am going to do exercises and return to school looking like a new me. I am going to work at not confusing my mother. I confuse her easily and most of the time I don't know how I do it. It's a bit to do with what I can't say, and her saying too much. She will announce something like,'I know you,' or, 'that's typical,' and immediately I can feel funny things growing out of my brain. I lose my temper and chuck a whole bucket load of anger out on her, when all I need is to say the one thing that is annoying me. Anyway, *this* summer I am going to get it right. She really isn't that bad. All my friends like her, say how great she looks, how generous she is. But they don't have to live with her full time. I am going to try. Seeing as Ed's away I don't have any excuses. It's Mum and me.

'Darling, do you have a moment?'

Do I have a moment? I have a million and one moments. I have trillions of seconds.

'Coming, Mum.'

I reckon that I could fly super-man style down our stairs. I like this house. I hated it when I first saw it, but now I like it. I like everything. Why? Because I am free.

'Gracious, you look happy.'

So does my mother as she sits beaming up at me, sitting on her swivel chair. The room used to be a linen cupboard. They must have had an awful lot of tea towels, because it's converted nicely into her study. She's recently acquired a computer thingy; since she went back to work she's become very technical. I have a good-looking mother. Once in a while it irritates me. She wears leggings and enormous T-shirts which she somehow manages never to shrink, and trainers. I know that I would look like an ape in drag if I collected all that lot together. She doesn't.

'What time did you get up?'

'Glorious twelve-thirty. I woke at seven, and then I woke at nine and then I ...'

'I suppose that's all right for the first week.' What does she mean, all right for the first week? This is the first week of many. I can choose. I can choose what I wear. I can choose where I go. I hate routine. I don't ever want to work from nine to five. I wonder is there a way to earn money while still getting loads of free time?

'I wish you didn't always wear black. Don't you get hot? I'm going to sit outside in a while. Why don't you put on something cool and ... '

This is a regular session with my mother. She's always wishing that I'd wear pretty clothes, a little bit of make-up, look the way she does. I don't want to. That's all. Anyway, it's freedom time and she and I are going to talk, to get on. I am not getting uptight for the next two thousand and sixteen hours; that's from now until the end of the holidays.

'I have something so thrilling to tell you.' She's really excited. Mum doesn't usually bounce and fizz like this.

'We're going to Greece? That'd be cool,' I wonder out loud. Then I'll really chuck myself at those ultra violet rays. I am going to stop being so serious about everything. I am going to lighten up and enjoy ...

'Don't say cool, Ness. It doesn't mean anything. All this cool and mega and bodacious. I don't know who thought up those dreadful expressions.'

This is the lecturer-parent speaking. Despite the outfit, she is still a middle-class English woman who is more into cave paintings than the latest film or what music I'm listening to, or whatever lovely collection of words expresses the right moment. All year long when I'm writing essays I have to put everything perfectly, try not to sound too friendly, write correctly. I don't have to do that for three whole months. Splendiferous!

'We're going to America. UCSC. It's in Santa Cruz. During the 'sixties and 'seventies a lot of the great thinkers were there. It will only be for a couple of months. When I was a student without a penny to my name I longed to travel to the States. I have been asked to co-ordinate three groups of students. They are all new English majors and we'll be covering Bacon and Shakespeare, then some of the Romantic poets.'

She has to be joking. How in heaven's name do you co-ordinate bacon and majors? She's under stress. All those exam papers are getting to her. I offered to mark some of them for her but she snapped my head off and told me to leave her in peace. There is no way that she can go to America. All her sentences are tumbling out. She isn't thinking straight, is she?

'We'll be able to tour around a bit, shop in Hollywood Boulevard, spot the film stars, maybe even take a trip to Mexico. Ness, we will have such fun.'

I am stunned. She is looking as if some man from Jupiter has told her there really is an after-life, and I am brain-dead. I cannot voice my disgust, I am ... speechless.

'We ought to have a bit of a re-think about what you'll take with you, clothes-wise.'

Dad, I need you.

'Our passport is organised. Oh, Ness, it's going to be marvellous.'

How can I skip the country when it's 'our' passport? Ed has a passport. I'm fourteen. I need one too. I must handle this situation with great care. When I'm surprised or confused or both I stammer a bit. I'm doing it now. I am trying ever so hard not to sound rude.

'Mum, I have so many ideas of my own. I ...' If I gulp then I won't rush at everything ... 'I would like it if we toured around here. Do you remember, we were going to go to Kerry?' And I know as I stutter and fluff that Mum's face is changing and I know I will end up being sent away, to my room. That way she can gather herself together before she gets extremely angry. She has a big temper, my Mum. It's controlled which makes it that bit more dangerous when it escapes.

I almost believed that things were going to be fine, good, great, super, wonderful. Well, there you are! You make all these promises to yourself about how you are going to change and they come to nothing.

All I said to Mum was, 'You're cracked. You cannot honestly believe that I am going away for the summer.' I thought about it, I didn't say it without thinking. I meant it. We had talked and made arrangements. She had liked them. I know she had.

Now her face crumbled. Her straight back and newly-cut long hair, feathered fringe and lashings of gloss on her lips suddenly seemed all fragile and false. She looked like one of those porcelain dolls she collects. This is the side of my mother that my friends don't see. No one understands.

'If you could, just once in a while see what I am trying to do for you.' She got up and paced around. 'I don't understand, I really thought you would be ... '

'Be what, Mum? I am only beginning to learn how to wake up and feel easy, to decipher what people are saying through their accents. I have only just learned the road signs. I have only recently worked out where the cheapest jeans can be found. I wonder about you, Mum. I really do.'

'What do you wonder about me? How dare you challenge me when all I want for you is the very best. I didn't have these opportunities when I was your age. Think it over. But I feel that it's not such a terrible burden.'

I've been thinking it over for hours. I ate my tea up here. I didn't want to be in the kitchen or any other part of the house where New Age Christopher Columbus might be lurking. I love the light outside my window. It's only a street light, but it's mine. I love my rabbit. Dad gave him to me for my First Communion. All my friends got watches. Dad gave me this fluorescent bunny. I love you, Dad.

<u>Six</u>

Why does grass have to grow so quickly? I mowed it last Friday. I almost dislocated my back so that I could earn money to pay for a video and packets of crisps as an end-of-term treat for my friends and me. And now look at it. It's like a meadow. Still, the daisies look pretty. It's a pity that you can't avoid them in the battle against the green stuff. I can still hear Mum's rotten music. I wish she'd play something decent. I can't even drown it out with my walkman. No batteries, no money and no prospect of cash for about three days. It's not fair. If I could get some baby-sitting or something everything would be all right. Apart from California.

It feels like a lifetime ago since we lived in England, Mum, Dad, Ed and me. Sunday visits from Gran were painful. Useful though. She gave us the odd fiver. She forgot my birthday this year. That's what happens when you move away. You are forgotten. And that's another reason why this Californian thing is such a bad idea. By the time we get back I'll have to begin again with everyone. It was an uphill battle last year. I couldn't go through it a second time.

How did Mum become so good at teaching? That's what I would love to know. There she was, an ordinary, acceptable wife and mother one minute, and the next ... Dad died. That's when everything stopped and went into a new orbit. Suddenly life became complicated. I think she likes throwing horrendous new situations at me. She must. First she moved me here. I like here, but it can still hurt when people laugh at me because I talk differently. And now she's doing it again.

She has a boyfriend, Peter. He's a vet. She says that he isn't a boyfriend, simply a friend who's a man but I know differently. It's thanks to him that she accepted the offer to teach at summer school in the States. I heard him.

'It will be good for you both.'

Huh!

'Let Nessie experience some of that marvellous hospitality. It will broaden her horizon.'

I'd like to flatten his face.

'She'll come back a real Yank.'

I hate that word, Yank. It's so insulting. I don't like being called a Brit. I bet my friends wouldn't take too kindly to being called Paddy. Yank! I couldn't use that word. That's the type he is, Peter, stupid let's-get-cosy, Fairhead. I pity any poor animal that comes his way. Maybe he'll get stuck in a field with a rampant ram. I'd enjoy that.

How come everyone precious is away when I need them? Clara would be able to put things right. I respect her. So does Mum. She has a way of getting straight to the centre of a situation. Clara doesn't mind what she says. It isn't that she's rude or offensive, but she is direct. Whenever I try to be like her I end up banished to my room. But she could explain rationally why this summer I need to build on the people I know here, not some pack of students I'll never see again. Trass would probably tell me that I should go. She's about the only person I know who has read and remembered the fourth commandment. But I can't honour my mother on this one.

29

'Jo said that any time I wanted a bed I was welcome.' As to whether I'm welcome for one sixth of the year I don't know.

If the music that I hear is anything to go by, Mum is already packing my bags and sorting out what new clothes I'll need for the trip. All those cellos, all those harps. She shouldn't play sad music. When I go in she will have had a giant crying session; she will want to talk about the old times, back to her selective remembering. It's all right sometimes, talking about the trips to Kew Gardens in the summer, and visits to Madame Tussaud's. But I am trying really hard to think forward. That's what Ed advised me to do. I can snuggle up with my thoughts at night-time but during the day I want to, if I can, get on with things. I know that this is what Dad would have told me. Ed is like Dad. That's why I wish he was here and not there. But Ed, like the rest of us, needs money and a break. There aren't any summer jobs in Cork at the moment, not unless you're very lucky. So, he's gone. I hope he comes back happier and ready to try again with Mum.

I'm going to go and see if she's in the mood for a chat.

'Chilled out' as Damien would put it. If she dares to try and persuade me to go with her just because she's sad I will have to get tough. Two can play at that game.

Seven

I don't believe it. It's June the twelfth and it's pouring rain. It looks like January. The weather cannot do this to me. Where has all the greenhouse effect gone? Has someone filled up the bald patches in the ozone layer? Yesterday I had to have two showers because I was hot and sweaty. Now I'll have to have another two to warm me up. Cork looks like it's in a shroud when it's damp and grey. This was not part of my summer plan.

'Stop scratching, cat!'

Puss, my fluffy companion, has fleas. Where does a cat who comes from a good home get fleas? Mum doesn't really like animals but she tolerates Puss, just. I have powdered, sprayed and put a collar on him, but he's still scratching. Giving me a filthy look he hops off the bed in a plume of dust — flea powder. I'll probably die in my sleep from inhaling the fumes. He's standing by the bedroom door waiting to be let out.

'Don't scratch in front of Mum. She'll probably drown you in sheep dip and shave you.'

He's gone. Mrs Dineen, our housekeeper, has organised a cat flap in the kitchen. Cat flaps are all very well but Puss insists on inviting his friends back late at night. One morning when I came into the kitchen there were three extra furry guests. One was sleeping on the new ceramic hob, one on top of the microwave and the third in a basket of clean washing. Puss, being the well-behaved chap he can be, was on a chair nestling into Mum's new blazer. I used up a roll of sticky tape trying to defur it. It didn't work. Puss's cat flap was battened down for a week. That's probably when he adopted the fleas, during his nights of exile in the garden.

'Telephone, Vanessa.'

Oh God! June the twelfth, it's raining and my mother is still being formal. Plus, I itch.

'Hi, it's me, Aideen.'

'Aideen, a friendly voice.'

'Trouble?'

'Not so you'd notice.'

I'm really glad. I haven't seen Aideen for ages. She lives in Bishopstown and our house is almost in the city. We are only a few short miles apart but it makes a difference. Her sister Sorcha is getting married. Aideen and I are bridesmaids and good friends.

'Have you heard the latest?' Aideen doesn't talk, she gallops. It's only when you look at her, almost lip read, that you can properly understand what she's saying.

'Crinolines, you know, big hoopy skirts, imagine *The King and I*, *Gone with the Wind*. Sorcha and Mum were drooling over bridal magazines and they saw this picture. It was called Southern Belle or something equally dorkish. Ness, I couldn't. Could you? What little street cred we have would be flushed down the loo. Think about it. Sorcha is meeting up with this dress designer friend of hers and she wants to introduce us to her because she's going to make our clobber as well. Ness, we have to do something, now. We have to make a plan.'

Sorcha is an air hostess. That's how I got to meet her, on the plane over from England. I was petrified and she was kind. Well, she used to be kind. Me in any kind of skirt amounts to cruelty to teenagers. I would make *Freddie's Nightmares* and *Alien* look like fairy tales. What has happened to Sorcha? She's very pretty, she's quite young and suddenly she isn't talking to me like a friend. She's now all grown up and responsible and talks to Mum. I loathe this age thing. If you're twelve you're a baby. If you're thirteen you're too young. If you're fourteen you're a child. When in heaven's name do I grow up? Is it magically, overnight? Suddenly, eighteen and I can drink, smoke, drive a car (if I can afford the insurance). Out of nowhere, trustworthy. I suspect there is a conspiracy against youth. In general, if you are young enough to remember only the last few years, you're lost. Sorcha might as well be my great, great grandmother over this wedding thing. I am bereaved. No joke! Sorcha's engagement means I have been deprived of someone special.

It was less than a year ago when I met Sorcha. Then, she wasn't in love; she was sympathetic. All this wedding business has made her go over the top. She came to our house with Rory, her man. She was kind of shiny and dizzy. Normally she doesn't stay for long, a quick cup of tea, a biscuit perhaps. But on this occasion, she talked for ages with Mum. That jerk, Peter, was drooling over a single bit of glass on her left hand. And Rory, you should see him. He isn't my answer to perfection. How can someone like Sorcha who was different, unique, become engrossed in crinolines and all the other rubbish that goes with weddings? That's why I'm only half-pleased I've been asked to be a bridesmaid. I ask you. I look like an elephant. I feel like a freak. Twelve months ago Sorcha would have understood.

Rory is a doctor. He works for WHO. At least I know what that stands for, unlike mother's UCSC. WHO is the World Health Organization, but Aideen and I still call him Doctor Who. I wouldn't have matched Sorcha up with him. He is so serious. If I were a computer dating service I would have found her someone funny, not Rory. He's the opposite to funny. I can get heavy about Ethiopia and Somalia. I still can't believe that all those television pictures are true. But Rory and Sorcha intend to change the world. After they are married they are flying out to South America where they will both be working with the very sick and the poor.

The way they go on about it, all smiles and optimism, makes me cringe. For a start, how will someone like Sorcha who loves make-up and fashion cope with no fresh water and thousands of children dumped because no-one can afford to look after them? At my age I know you can't do it, just hop into a situation. I'm convinced that she's making a mistake, and is she listening? No, she is not. She's glowing with excitement about this rotten wedding. As for Rory, he's odd, he talks about favellas or whatever the places are called as if he's about to stay in The Hilton or The Ritz. I know a favella is a hopelessly poor place. How will Sorcha of-the-expensive-perfume-and-the-scooped-up-hair cope with all that poverty? Worse still, will I, ten years from now make the same brutal mistake? Uuugh ... I'm not sure I want to grow up.

Eight

I have rung the Kellehers about a million times. No reply. I've tried thought transference. Maybe if Damien knows I'm worried he'll magically appear. That's how desperate I am. Mum is adamant that I am going with her, and Sorcha is determined that Aideen and I are to look like flying saucers at the end of August as we trip down the aisle behind her. All this cannot be happening at once.

Luckily Aideen is coming over tonight. She's having problems with her mother too. She had been grounded for ten days because she didn't return from an end-of-term get together until after one in the morning. Honestly, she did ring home to say she was going to be late. She got a lift back and apparently her mother was waiting in the kitchen pacing around like a caged platypus and ranting on about how she thought Aideen was drugged, dead, drowned etc. I suppose it must be scary though. *We* know where we are when we're out, and *we* understand who we're with, but the oldies sit around waiting for the worst to happen.

'Nessie, are you ready to give me a hand?'

That's Mrs Dineen. Now she's really ancient but she has more sense than a lot of people I know.

'I checked the labels, Ness, not a drip or drop of animal fat or flesh in sight.'

I'm a vegetarian, and Mrs D has always treated it as a challenge to her cooking talents, not an additional headache, which is how Mum sees it. We're stuffing spicy pitta breads with a Mexican mixture.

'Mrs Dineen?'

'Yes, Ness.'

'Are you around this summer?'

'For most of it. I have to visit my mother at some point, but that will only be for a day or two.'

'I don't want to go away, that's all. I want to do all the things I planned, not something that Mum has suddenly foisted on me.'

It's not fair my asking Mrs D to look after me, I know, not that I need looking after, but you never know. She's a persuasive person and she might be able to make Mum change her mind.

'Ness, that is between your mother and you. Why don't you talk it over with her again?'

Talk it over. That would be fine if Mum knew how to listen. Aideen was saying the same thing. She tried to explain to her mother about how gross we'd both look as stand-ins for Little-Bo-Peep. Her mother had a fit and said that not only was Sorcha putting her under unendurable pressure by only giving her three months to prepare for the wedding, but that now Aideen was behaving like a spoilt brat. What does she need more time for, anyway? According to Aideen all the right hotels are booked out, the cake won't be mature and her Dad's had to take out a loan to pay for the wrong hotel, the immature cake and three dresses that only one of us, Sorcha, wants to wear.

'I'm going to try the Kellehers' number again, Mrs Dineen.'

'I'll give you a call when I need the dressing for the salad. Yours always tastes better than mine.'

If Mrs D and I were left alone during the summer we'd have a great time. We could go to Ballycotton to see her mother. She's ninety-four; ninety-four years! I

36

don't think I'd want to be around that long. Knowing my mother she'll live to be a hundred and ninety and she'll still be disorganising my life.

'Hi, Jo. Ness here ... I'm fine.'

I can't tell her over the phone that I'm suicidally miserable.

'May I speak to Damien? Oh, what time will he be back?' He's gone into work with his father. How could he!

'No, nothing special, I was planning ...'

'You are planning nothing, young lady. You and I are going to sit down and sort out our differences.' I would like to tell my mother not to listen into my personal conversations. I wouldn't mind but she takes all her own 'phone calls in her study. Whenever idiot Peter Fairhead rings he always makes the same joke.

'Page me through to the Presidential Suite.'

He actually thinks it's funny. Ed keeps telling me that Peter is good for Mum, that he cheers her up on a lonely day. Maybe the pair of them will go to California and leave me in peace.

'Will you ask him to ring me when he gets back? Thanks Jo. Jo ...'

I was going to say that I'd like to come and talk to her, but she's gone. Anyway, she'd say the same as Mrs Dineen, talk it over. Only reasonable parents talk things over. The unreasonable ones end up running countries and ruining other people's lives.

Nine

Mum and I are walking over to the Kellehers. Jo is my last hope. As a friend to both of us maybe she will be able to sort out why I don't need an American tan and why I do need to stay with them. It would be so good. Everything about their house is different from ours. The noise for a start, the sense of being in the middle of an ant hill instead of our quiet existence. It must be like a permanent party. Plus I can talk to Jo and Marc. Marc is one of the kindest people I know. He works as an electrical engineer, but where he's happiest is at home. He never stops building things, or doing stuff to the house. But the real reason I want to stay is Jo. She understands me. She doesn't go on and on about the clothes I wear or the music I listen to. She knows how to let her family breathe. That's why Damien is such a together person. My Mum studied psychology when she was a student, but I don't think she has a clue. She won't let me be me. Jo will.

The other reason why it suddenly seemed the answer to all my problems is that Enda is away. If she was still there I wouldn't have even thought about it, but little miss perfect is taking a trip to Disney World with her parents and then on to St Tropez. Typical! Enda's Dad is some big executive with business interests from Cork to Sidney and backing into China. You should see him. He wears so much gold he clinks. Sometimes I feel sorry for Enda because she doesn't really seem to belong anywhere.

Please let Jo be able to sort this mess out. She's

brilliant. She isn't like an adult. You can talk about anything to her and she isn't shocked. It's not that she's trying to be young or 'in' with you. It's just how she is. She's done a lot to make Mum relax.

There's so much to learn about a new country. Everything is smaller here. In some ways that's good, in others it isn't. I'm always bumping into Mum's friends for a start. I felt it when I first came here, that I couldn't get away from things. I can't cope with the States at the moment. I said that to Mum. It would be too different. I need to get used to one thing at a time.

Mum has started smoking again. I wish she hadn't. She was sitting there behind a great bank of grey. It's going to wreck her skin all over again. She's getting wrinkly.

'What do you want to do, Ness?'

She was wearing her defeated face. I hate that. I hate to think that I have brought on that look, and yet that's what I've been trying to do for days.

'May I stay at Jo's for some of the time and in our own house for the rest? Ed will be back at the end of July. I'll be fine, Mum. I can't face all those new people. I feel lost.'

And she began to cry. Please don't cry, Mum, please. She is so tough and so soft. We're walking over to the Kellehers to see if Jo will have me. I feel like an orphan all over again. I feel like a parent decimator. I feel guilty and excited. Oh, Mum!

Mum and Jo are great friends. I don't know how Jo puts up with my mother. Jo's down to earth. She has to be with all those different personalities demanding attention. Mum can be a bit of a poser. It's not her fault, I suppose. She's trying to be all sorts of people, a mother, a father, a friend. I don't want my mother as a friend, but I do want her as someone I can trust.

39

Just as we get to their front door Mum says, 'Now, Ness, don't force the issue. If Jo is planning other things for the summer and you don't fit into those plans, you'll have to accept it.'

'I understand.'

Why does she have to say the obvious? It's like during school time she always asks if I've done my homework, or if I ate my lunch. I have a brain. If I don't eat my lunch I get hungry, if I don't do my homework I'll get into trouble. If she were to ask me something interesting then I wouldn't snap answers back at her. Not only do I wish that I could trust my mother, I wish that she'd trust me.

Here goes.

'Alex, Ness, come on in. The kettle's on and Ophelia has been baking since we spoke on the phone. Toby, can you take Tom? Thanks. Now come on down.'

Toby was always tall but over the last few months he's grown huge. As he marches off down the hallway with Tom on his shoulders they have to duck under arches; otherwise poor Tom would be as headless as Cassie's favourite doll, Batty.

Let me put you in the picture, age-wise, that is. Marc and Jo are in their thirties. Jo got married when she was twenty. For anyone else it would have been disastrous, but, miraculously, maybe because of the children, Marc and Jo still like each other. Damien is coming up to sixteen. I wish he'd get back. I want so much to see him just in case I'm shipped off abroad without notice. I feel like a tragic heroine. Toby is galloping towards fifteen. Ophelia is almost thirteen. Sophie is eleven. Sophie is the dreamer of the family. If her Mum asks her to get the cornflakes from the cupboard Sophie will probably turn on the empty washing machine. Then there's Darragh; he's ten. Darragh, unlike the others, is consciously super-trendy. He has grown his fringe so that it touches his chin. His jeans are always perfectly frayed. He is going to be a heart breaker when he gets bigger. Hugh is seven and seems to be perpetually without teeth; as one grows into place another drops out. I'd forgotten about the tooth fairy until I came to this house. Cassie and Chris are twins. They're four, but they are very definitely the product of different eggs! Chris is sweet and quiet. Cassie is crazy. There's nothing she likes more than a good hand-to-hand fight with her brother. Lastly there's Tomas. He's almost two and they all share in looking after him. Almost all. Cassie's attentions are a bit of a liability.

Damien and Toby couldn't be more different. Toby is about six foot two and very athletic. He loves rugby and goes to a school where there are lots of sports, the same school as Ed goes to, in fact. Damien is not quite as tall. He has long floppy hair and a face that's always moving. If I were to choose to go out with anyone I'd go out with Damien. But as I have trouble understanding myself I don't think it would be fair to launch myself on another human being. Maybe it would. I don't know. I'm full of all these good intentions until he says something complimentary, then I wonder if it wouldn't be perfect to say, 'Yes, we're going out.' But what difference does it make! More confusion.

'California! Alex you are making me envious thinking about it.' Jo's joyous outburst to my beloved trouble-making mama, alias Alexandra Rose Carter, was not what I wanted to hear.

'Cass, please don't keep taking Tom's carrot ...

41

Cassie!' Jo is bi/tri/ambidextrous. She can be discussing an article in the newspaper, peeling potatoes and washing Hugh's face while rescuing Cassie from inside the fridge, all at the one time.

'It is exciting, Jo. The young people I will be teaching are about to begin their English major. It could be useful in the future were I to consider a sabbatical abroad.'

That's made me sit up. She hasn't mentioned that bomb-shell before. I'm going to yell. No, I'm not. I'm going to sit tight. Ophelia's raspberry flan is good. I'm going to be the size of a whale, I've eaten so much. What's a sabbatical? I'll look it up when I get home. It sounds like a very tricky and extremely messy operation.

'But there is an unexpected problem.'

Mum is looking pointedly at me. I mustn't blush.

'Ness seems to think that two months away from her friends will make life difficult next term. I've tried reasoning with her.'

Oh thank you God that Toby grabbed Tom from Cass and they've gone into the garden, that Ophelia is watching TV in the corner and that Sophie has drifted upstairs. A double treble thank you that Damien isn't here. I would die if he'd heard Mum say that. I said it to her in confidence. She didn't realise how much effort and time I'd put into working out what was wrong. And now she's blabbing it out like a soup recipe. I wasn't being difficult. Why does everything that I do have to be difficult in her eyes? I was being honest.

Ten

'Ness, any spare toothbrush around?' Aideen always forgets something when she stays. Then she always leaves something behind when she goes. Tonight she's really happy. Until today she was wearing double train tracks on her teeth. A few months ago, when she was here for the weekend she really cried. That is not Aideen's style. Some freak at school was calling her 'choo choo'. Do you get it? Train tracks, train, choo? It made her self-conscious and sad. It's all very well to have these dentists stringing our mouths up with metal, but I reckon it's a bit like telling a baby that teething doesn't hurt. Braces hurt your mouth and your feelings as well. But the good news is she's onto a single line, and she can take it out some of the time. Brilliant!

'It's great not spitting everywhere. I might even miss all those chunks of mince trapped underneath,' Aideen announced in the kitchen. Mrs Dineen was most sympathetic. She wears dentures so she too has teeth trouble.

'Now, tell me all about this afternoon at the Kellehers.' It's as well we have strong floors. Aideen lands on my bed from a hurtled three-foot jump and everything shakes.

I try to look heart-broken but I can't. My face is breaking out in a grin.

'Jo really tried to persuade me. I'm not sure if she meant it or did it for Mum's sake. She kept saying what a brilliant opportunity it was. How it was a chance in a lifetime. I panicked. I thought that I was about to lose a second friend. First of all Sorcha and then Jo. But it's all right. I can stay there until Ed gets back in July. Mum spoke to Mrs D. She's going to keep an eye on the house and live in for some of the time while Mum's away. The cat can come to the Kellehers too. It's going to be fine.'

I suddenly noticed the look on Aideen's face.

'What's wrong?'

'What you said about Sorcha ...'

'Aideen, I'm sorry. I wasn't thinking.'

'But you're right. She isn't around most of the time. When she is, *he's* with her. She used to come and sit in my bedroom and tell me about where she'd been, who she'd met. Now it's all Rory this and Rory that. We used to talk; like when things get a bit difficult with the parents, she'd listen to my side. Now she's engaged and there's no room left for me.'

Giving Aideen a hug I try to think what it would be like if Ed suddenly acted grown up and superior. It would be like losing a limb.

We have to meet the wedding dress designer next week. The day after I move into the Kellehers in fact. Her name is Eleanora Stratton. If she's anything like her name and her venue, The Imperial Hotel, it's going to be diabolical.

'Where did Sorcha pick her up?' I mean, with a name like that, she sounds like a reject from a soap opera.

'They went to school together. She used to be Eleanora Monks. Then she met up with the Honorable Piers Stratton.' They definitely belong in one of those thick books that you see at airports. I need more information.

'It's a bit sad. He was working for a bank in

44

Singapore ...' This is all too exotic, and what is so sad about banking in Singapore? '... And he kind of went off with someone else. So poor old Eleanora is running this little dress shop in Dublin by day, selling other designers' clothes; then at night she designs her own gear. I can't remember her very well but Sorcha thought that she ought to give an old friend the chance to make her the dress of a lifetime.'

Aideen and I pull identical faces simply thinking about the dress of a lifetime. Forever ... Now that *is* a frightening thought!

'Won't you miss your Mum? Two months is a long time.'

'Aideen, I am going to be at the Kellehers. Of course I won't miss her. I won't miss Peter either. He won't be hanging around until Ed gets back. Just think, I'll be a part of all the fun the Kellehers have. I hate leaving their house. Coming home always makes me feel down. It's so boring here. Nothing happens. Unlike Mum Jo doesn't go on about crumbs on the work surface, or moan about shoes not put side-by-side in a cupboard. She's much more interested in how everyone is, not if they're making perfect impressions and developing into proper little housewives. Mum is so stiff by comparison.'

Aideen is looking doubtful. I don't know why. It's going to be great. I feel happy. I hope Mum will be safe. What am I thinking about? It's her choice to go transatlantic. I can't wait for next week.

Eleven

Mum has freaked. She's been recording traditional Irish music for the last three days. If I hear any more 'diddley-ay-di-di' I will curl up and diddley die. It's all Mrs Dineen's fault. She has been lending Mum records and tapes that look as if they are the originals Noah chucked out of the ark when he was advised it was about to sink. I told Mum that I thought it all sounded the same, at which point she informed me that I had killed my musical sensibilities. Did I ever have any? Then she suggested that all the 'noise' I listen to was probably destroying my brain. How bad! Her new craze for jigs and reels is temporary hopefully.

'The students will like it,' she explained. Only if they're demented!

'There's a lot of interest in Irish culture in the States.'

I'm sure there is. I thought she was going over there to teach literature. Now she's suddenly turning into a Celtic groupie.

'When I get back ...' You haven't gone yet, but you will soon. '... I thought I might attend set-dancing classes.'

Maybe Mum's right. Perhaps my hearing is going.

'It's wonderful exercise and great fun. How about you and Ed joining us?'

'Us?' Shock-horror, she can't be thinking about dancing with Peter, can she?

'Mrs Dineen and I thought we'd give it a whirl.'

The prospect of my mother and Mrs D whirling anywhere sent me racing over to the Kellehers. I'm prepared to settle-in in Ireland, make friends and all that, but Mum appears to be taking root. She is a combination of an over-joyed and over-protective mother towards me at the moment. In a funny sort of way I think that I might have quite liked this trip of hers. It's too late now, but in my enthusiasm to get through all the things planned for this summer, I overlooked an important fact. Nobody, except for Aideen, is available. Damien and Toby are working. Why didn't someone warn me that whole families take off in droves during June and July? Anyway, I've checked with Jo about whether I should bring my duvet and covers. She took me up to Enda's room and showed me where I could put my clothes when I arrive and assured me there were enough blankets and sheets to stock a small hotel. Even so, I think I'll bring my own quilt. It's got a familiar feel.

I've packed two hold-alls. Puss definitely suspects something strange is about to happen. He keeps prowling around my bulging sports bag and miaowing pathetically. He probably thinks there's a store of cat food in there and wants to check the sell-by date. Most of the rooms have been tidied and are ready to be shut for the big send-off, which is only forty-eight hours away. Ed's sleeping quarters (to call where he normally resides a bedroom would be a sin!) are in a state of such cleanliness that he will probably need to be inoculated on his return.

'Ness, Nessie.'

A happy mother is calling. Leaping onto the landing she is running up the stairs two by two. She's fit, there's no denying that. By rights her lungs should be little sacks of solid fuel, but without so much as a wheeze she is suggesting we go out for lunch.

'Can we go to the Indian restaurant?' I want to know.

'Not today. I've found you somewhere special.' I wonder what it's like to be middle-aged?

'Put a move on. Why don't you get changed?' Now I know!

'How about that little sun-dress I bought for you.'

'Oh, Mum.' Sighing, which normally means I'm not going to change my mind, I do it anyway. In a short while I will be with Jo and Marc and Damien and the others. Then maybe we'll all go to the Indian restaurant and I can wear whatever I choose. Whoever invented sun-dresses didn't have a spotty back and moles. How do mothers do it — make you feel guilty?

'Well, what do you think?'

I think it is verging on amazing that I wasn't stopped and arrested for indecent exposure.

'Do you like it?'

We are sitting in a vegetarian restaurant. It's in a renovated old warehouse by the quay and it has the best veggie menu I have ever seen. (Not that I've seen many.)

'Thank you, Mum, for thinking.' And I mean it.

'Don't slouch, Ness.'

Don't spoil it, Mum. But the restaurant was a lovely idea.

Twelve

At last we're here. All the packing and the phone calls and the dark looks are over. Mum has told me twenty thousand times to help at the Kellehers, has reminded me how generous they are, how kind they are. I know, Mum, I know. That is why I am looking forward so much to being with them. Wait until Clara and Trass find out. They will be so envious. I feel lucky again. Mum's pinned a list on my bedroom mirror of things I mustn't forget, things like, check that the freezer is working; it shudders occasionally and stops. I have to collect her letters and put them in her study, organise someone to sweep the chimney and get Puss's injections done. I didn't think that she would think of that one. Good old Mum.

I like Cork Airport. Even since I've come to live here it's got bigger, but it's nothing like Heathrow in London. Heathrow is frightening. Mum was always on the watch for someone who was about to kidnap us there. I'm kind of fat at the moment. My legs look like I've borrowed them from a rhino, so only someone heavily into wild life would abduct me. But I love all the bustle and the smiles and the grannies waiting by the windows as the planes land. Then they leap up like two-year-olds when they spot their own familiar person. There's a lot of that here, saying goodbye and welcome back. A lot of people work away from Ireland. No jobs! Help, what am I going to do when I'm twenty?

Jo organised the bigger ones to take care of the

smallies back at their house. So there's Damien and myself and Marc and Jo. And mother. Mum is all glamour this morning as we wait to say goodbye. She has her sun specs on top of her head, her hair is tied back with a scrunchy, and even though she has lines around her face she looks good. You can see people following her with their eyes, admiring looks all round. I suppose she's slim and all that, but I still wish she wasn't being noticed. She's my mother for heaven's sake!

'Ness, I'll ring tomorrow. I promise.'

I'm taller than she is. That's one ambition achieved, but if I continue to grow I'm going to put bricks on my head at night.

'Did you hear me, pet?'

Poor Mum, she only ever says pet when she's in a panic.

'I said read it when you get back.'

Handing me a lumpy envelope she looks misty and makes me feel the same.

'We've time for coffee. Shall I get you two cokes?' Marc asks as he escorts Jo and Mum to a table.

'Let's look at magazines,' I suggest to Damien.

Leafing through *Hello* I wonder where all these glamorous people get their money from. Some of the houses are ridiculous. How do they sleep at night? Not only would they have to worry about who might break in to steal their goodies, but how could anyone wear a tiara when someone else couldn't even afford a cup of tea? Ages ago Dad said I was going to turn into a cause bore. And that was before I gave up meat and avoided too many newspapers. I got to a point when I couldn't read all the sad bits. Mrs Dineen goes on about rays of hope, but she has this lovely blind way of looking at things. I think I'll be an environmentalist when I leave school. That way I might persuade people who dump rubbish in rivers and on the roads to think again. Or maybe I'll ...

'Did you say something? Are you all right?' Damien asks, squeezing my elbow.

'Of course.' I sound harsh. I don't feel it. He's lovely the way he un-self-consciously holds onto people. They all do it at their house, touch, that is. We aren't like that in ours. Once in a while, when you really need someone, Ed can do it. But Mum isn't a touch person. She's just touchy!

'Dad's calling us over.'

It's all right now. The intercom and the children charging around waiting impatiently to begin their holidays remind me that mine are also about to start. I feel odd, kind of thrilled. I've wanted freedom for so long and it's about to happen. There will be just me and the sort of family you dream about. Only this isn't a dream.

Ed made things perfect. He rang last night to wish Mum luck. That was a nice thought. I was trying to persuade Puss into a cardboard box with a tin of cat food at the time, a practice run for this morning. I have to collect him on the way home. Ed sounded fine. He says he's lost a load of weight because the work is hard but that he'll have enough cash saved to keep him going for the next year. I didn't speak to him for long. He grunted something inaudible about my not going with Mum but didn't seem too annoyed. Heck, he's where he wants to be and I am doing what I want.

'Ness, Jo says that at anytime if you get home-sick you can ring Tony and Fran.'

My Aunt and Uncle in England. I would need to be

dying of the plague and about to be burnt at the stake before I'd ring them.

'I'll make sure you have my number tomorrow. Now any problems and ...'

'They're calling passengers for the flight to Dublin, Alex. Here, let me take your bags.'

Marc gathers her hold-all, her handbag, her sunglasses, which are on the table.

'Please, Nessie ...'

She's pleading with me, despite the fact that all my clothes, my underwear and my Clearasil are at the Kellehers. She imagines I'm going to climb on board the plane with her. Handing her a copy of the sort of book she used to read when she didn't know how clever she could be, I back off.

'Have a fabulous trip, Mum. I'll see you in August.'

Watching her and Marc and Jo walking towards the departure lounge I wonder if I should have given her a kiss. I know how to talk to my friends. I know how to hold Puss until he squirms away disgusted, but I just couldn't kiss my mother in front of all those people, in front of Damien.

Thirteen

My head is spinning and turning. I hate it when it does that. It means I'm not going to be able to sleep for hours. It is already one in the morning. I've turned the light back on. I miss Puss. Jo has put him in an outhouse. He looked very miserable when I left him. I think maybe Mrs Dineen was right. She offered to take care of him at our house. She said that she would pop in and make sure that he was all right and said that I could do the same during the day. If I were to lose Puss I don't think I could cope.

It's odd. I forgot to check with Jo about the cat and the kitchen. She loves him dearly but Hugh has asthma so he can't have cat's fur around the place. That's why he has his slimy turtles for pets. I'll have to take Puss home tomorrow. I miss the street light outside my bedroom window.

This is very definitely an Enda-type room. The bedspread matches the wallpaper which is covered in delicate pale blue flowers. It looks cold beside my cavorting Thumper and Bambi wallpaper. I don't think I like this room and I feel too tired to start diving around changing the covers. Anyway my quilt is somewhere downstairs. I'd never be able to find it.

Stop that, Vanessa Carter. Stop feeling sorry for yourself. Tomorrow I'm meeting up with Aideen, and the eighty pounds that was in with the letter and card from Mum means I am well set-up for the next eight weeks. That was sweet of Mum. I thought she might give me a few pounds but eighty ... It was the card that confused me.

At first I thought she'd made a mistake. The writing was unfamiliar and the card was faded. There was just a J signed at the bottom. And then it dawned on me. I read the words first time over and thought, God! That's the mushiest thing I've ever read. It almost made me feel sick. I thought Mum had flipped or something. Then I looked at the writing, a bit closer. It was lucky I was here in Enda's room. If I'd been with any of the others they wouldn't have known what to do with me. I sobbed. I'm still having the odd hiccup ... I'm going to give up getting upset for Lent.

The J stands for John and this is what my Dad wrote to my Mum heavens knows when. The card is like vellum, scalloped round the sides and it's a washed grey/green. Very 'sixties.

Though the sea erode, the rivers dry, the mountains slide, the eagle fly, I will love you Rose until I die.

Isn't that the most beautifully sick thing you've ever read? Then I read Mum's letter.

My dear Ness,

I miss you already, I'm afraid. But you are absolutely right. This is not the time to ask you to resettle, even if only for a short time. You and Ed are turning into such brave young people. It is hard not to be proud of you both. I enclosed the little verse from your father because it is special to me. Keep it safe until I get back. Do all those things that you have planned.

With my love,
Mum.

PS Your father always had trouble making Alex

rhyme with anything. That's where the nickname
Rosie came from. Love you Ness XXX

I wonder if Mum thinks I'm too tough to be touched by something like that, or did she know how much it would affect me? My earless rabbit who has shared my bed since I was six is looking forlorn. Maybe I'll get Eleanora to fashion him some experimental velvet ears. I'm dreading meeting up with that woman tomorrow. She will be glamorous and Aideen and Sorcha will look beautiful and I'll look huge.

I hate even admitting it to myself, but sometimes I'm quite envious of Aideen. I couldn't say it. But it's true. She has grown her hair long. It's black and sleek. In a fit of madness I had mine permed. I imagined all these waves cascading. I look like a Bedlington terrier. Even Damien laughed. And that's something else that's bothering me. I thought we'd stay up late tonight, watch films, do stuff. But at eleven-thirty on the dot, Marc began turning off lights.

'Work tomorrow, my friends,' he said.

He put his hand out to Jo but she said, smiling, 'Give me five minutes. I want to talk to Damien and Ness.'

I had visions of some big sex talk. You know, now that you two are alone in the house together (well, as alone as you can be with ten others), I feel I ought to remind you of your moral responsibility. All that nonsense. Instead, 'Damien.'

He looked down at her. She's very little. His legs are ridiculous in Bermudas; they are too long and too hairy. And he's taken to wearing a pony-tail for the summer. He'll have to chop it once he's back to school.

'Could you please curb your language in front of the little ones and Ness too, come to think of it. You manage to most of the time when Enda's around. The rules haven't changed. Hugh only borrowed fuse wire. It didn't take all those expletives to show your disapproval, did it?'

Laughing, Damien bent down and kissed the top of his mother's head.

'I'll try,' he said, winking at me.

I should have said a proper goodbye to Mum.

Fourteen

Breakfasting with Damien and family is an unusual experience, to say the least. Gone, my imaginings of a lie-in until my head pounded. We were all sitting round the table at eight-thirty. Jo was concerned at my not having slept too well. She even suggested that maybe I ought to see the doctor because I look pale. Then Cass piped up.

'I heard her crying. You can have Batty.'

With that she slid off her chair and rummaging through one of the twenty or so bags she keeps her treasures in, she produced her doll, still without it's head. Luckily no one heard, or, as I suspect, no one picked up on the crying bit.

'There,' she said, slapping it into my cereal, as if this was how she always topped someone's muesli.

'Sorry, Ness, and thank you, Cass, but go easy, poppet; you'll drown poor Batty.'

That was it. Jo, cloths in hand, one for me, one for the table, began mopping up.

Tomas has a novel method of getting food from his bowl to his mouth: with two fat hands he hoists up the bowl and sucks. The noise is like a bath being drained. Marc, in a smart suit, presides quietly, opening the jam or the marmalade, buttering bread and remaining totally clean throughout.

'You take the bus today,' Jo calls as she turns sausages. Darragh and Hugh live on sausages and beans and bananas, nothing else, according to Jo.

'The bus' sounds cruel, but the bus is the family car.

It's an old transit van that Marc and Toby and Damien mess with when they're not messing with televisions, electric guitars, and, most recently, computers.

'What time is Aideen calling round?' Damien wants to know.

'She isn't. I said I'd meet her at half eleven outside the hotel.' I don't know why he's frowning. Unless, maybe he was hoping to see Aideen. That would be perfect, me liking Damien to distraction, and he waiting around for Aideen!

'Sophie ... That's enough milk. Oh, Sophie.' With a big sigh Jo gets going with the cloth again. 'I sometimes wonder where you go to when you gaze into the distance.' There's something in Jo's tone of voice that makes me look up and stop thinking horrible thoughts about Aideen. Sophie is eating away as if nothing has happened. She didn't notice that the milk was slopping all over the place or that there was an edge to her mother's voice.

Voices are like that. The slightest difference to a familiar sound and you know that something is wrong. But we all know that Sophie wanders away sometimes. It's as if she has a different land to go to. She's a tiny bit deaf. That's because she had measles when she was a baby. But people who know her raise their voice a bit when they're talking to her. Jo definitely looks concerned.

I remember, only a few months ago, I wandered into the kitchen here. The boys were upstairs practising with the band. I don't know where the smallies were, probably with the girls, and Jo was all by herself in a silent kitchen. Most unusual.

'Is it all right if I get a glass of water?' I asked.

58

'Of course. There's fresh juice there if you want it ... Ness, thank you.'

I knew immediately that she was saying something a bit more.

'Thank you? What have I done except eat you out of house and home?'

'You've worked wonders with Damien.'

Me, I adore him from a distance and I want to keep him as my friend. But that's all I've done.

'When he was little he was painfully shy. Then, there were all the others. Toby being so close in age, they stuck together.' Damien? Shy?

'He was totally out of his depth at national school. He was never any good at football, or any kind of ball game, come to think of it. And then when he went to secondary school, he met up with Mr Fahy, the computer science teacher. It was like pulling back heavy shutters. He began to blossom.'

Damien, the boy that everyone wants to get to know, used to be a wallflower, a recluse. He's so popular now, and noisy, and demonstrative, and kind ...

'Then you came along and really made him come out of himself.'

I did?

'Enda used to be so clingy.'

Cousin Enda, who used to hang onto Damien's arm like a limpet. I thought they were going out together.

'But since you've been on the scene she's a lot less possessive.'

Great! I'm everybody's friend. Friend, but that's it ...

I'm suddenly pulled back into the present.

'My goodness, Ness, you look as dreamy as Sophie.' Jo's looking directly at me, cup in hand, eyes smiling.

'Let's go and feed Puss. He'll think you've forgotten him.' Ophelia, grabbing the cat food and a saucer, heads for the back door.

'Thanks for breakfast, Jo,' I shout back as I leave.

'That'll be a first for Mum, someone thanking her for breakfast,' Toby calls after us, teasing.

I don't really know Ophelia at all. She's starting at our school in September. She doesn't look old enough but she'll be thirteen at the end of October. She's like her Mum, little and dark, and like the boys, loves music, only she plays the violin, quietly. Once in a while Toby persuades her to 'fiddle'. It sounds professional. Marc joins in on the bodhrán; that's a drum affair which you bash with what looks like a chicken leg. It's all very ethnic and noisy and fun.

I wonder if boys confide in friends the way girls do? It's not that I go into anything too deep with Trass but she'd understand why I'm feeling so miffed about everything. My period is due. I have a gigantic spot on my chin that looks like a mountain. My shorts feel tight. I washed my bra with a pair of track suit trousers so what should be snow white is dirty grey. To think I used to long for all these changes! I ought to warn Ophelia before it's too late. Enjoy being twelve; anything thereafter is complicated.

Fifteen

'So you are Vanessa. Hi! Greetings and I adore that hair. It's almost too much.'

Hang about, wait a moment. I only knocked on the door of room eighteen of the Imperial Hotel. Maybe mother is right. Cork is becoming more cosmopolitan. Who is this person? She can't be, she can't ...

'Elly, meet Ness. Ness, my old friend Elly.'

Sorcha is giving me a big welcome, and Aideen is bouncing on the bed and asking if she can ring room service.

'Three tequilas, three lemons and a bucket of salt,' she requests as she pretends to ring on the in-house phone. Oh Aideen. No wonder Damien likes you. You're bubbly, bouncy and crazy.

'Lovely to meet you. Who did your hair? It's the best.' It is? I can't even remember if I dragged my fingers through it this morning, never mind combed it.

'What I envisage is a beauty and the beast type thing. Rory is beast enough, so we'll have three beauties. Okay?'

I don't know what she's talking about. I like the beast bit though. Aideen is grinning madly at me and Sorcha doesn't seem bothered. How can I describe Eleanora? All my visions of sleek elegant suave sophistication have been thrown in with the rest of the rubbish in the river. Eleanora is under five feet. This is a small person. She has a shaved head, but for a curtain of hair round the back. This woman is different, with a capital D. No wonder the honourable Piers found another. He was

61

probably brought up on some draughty Scottish estate, and will be riding with hounds after he's finished his stint in Singapore. I wonder if she always looked like this? Or maybe on the wedding night she shaved her head as a surprise. I am shocked, I am ...

'I tried to persuade our air hostessy to let you wear ballet docs.'

Ballet docs? Aideen is shrugging her shoulders, and Sorcha is actually ringing room service. She probably needs a strait jacket for her friend. No, it's pots of coffee and sandwiches and cake. If my mother meets the famous Elly she'll faint. She will.

'But boring old Sorcha wants to be trad. I ask you, commissioning me to do the right thing!'

I think Sorcha has made a rather large mistake in being charitable towards an old friend. Right now a crinoline sounds the perfect bridesmaid dress. Elly could easily design us into something topless or bottomless and the crowning glory would be us, bald, except for a fringe.

'Measurements we'll do later. Aids.'

She is calling Aideen Aids? I don't think that Elly, or whatever Sorcha calls her, is going to be left standing if she says that too often.

'Eleanora, the name's Aideen. I like it that way. Right?' I knew it. Aideen never abbreviates her name. She likes it just the way it is.

'Okey dokey. Give me your version of what you want and I'll give you mine.'

This lady is infectiously hard skinned. What is she wearing? I don't like my reaction to all this. I feel like I've slipped into my mother's skin. I am shocked. I am surprised. I am old fashioned. Eleanora has a husky voice. It's got a different lilt to it. It sounds a bit like

Liverpool but it's Dublin. She is wearing minuscule shorts and a string vest. And I suppose what she calls ballet docs; they're suede and laced half way up her leg. I don't know how she travelled but I hope it wasn't on public transport.

'Sorcha and I already know what we're doing with her. I will lose all my regular customers if they find out but I'll do it anyway.'

Her regular customers can only go out when it's dark.

'Colours, Nessie. Favourites?'

It's a question. I know it is.

'Black.' It's the truth. I like black. That way I never have to think about what Mum calls co-ordination. Black goes with everything.

'Could you open out the colour chart a weeny bit, just for Sorcha?'

She screws up her totally unmade-up-face and I have to keep reminding myself that this is a nice person, an old friend of Sorcha, a dress designer. I'm confused.

'Grey.' I'm looking around trying to find something to concentrate on. Aideen is opening the door. Food is at hand. If I eat something maybe I will be able to concentrate.

'You're purple. Very definitely purple. And you're violet. Oh yes, two little pansies.'

Is she insulting us?

'Silk or leather?

How did I get involved in all this? How did Sorcha go to school with this person? I can't wear a silk dress. I can't wear leather either.

'Leggings?'

All her questions are thrown into thin air. Sorcha is unphased. What has Sorcha chosen? Rory is not going to like this. He is a very formal guy.

'I hate frills,' she says.

That's obvious. Eleanora belongs in the garden of Eden, two or three carefully designed fig leaves and she'd be as happy as a mouse in a cheese factory.

'One concession. White bodies.' White bodies? Are we to be painted? To think that I was worried about my grey bra.

'You mean body stockings, I assume?' asks Sorcha, pouring coffee and handing a cup into my shaking hand.

'What else. Mind if I smoke?'

After Eleanora, I am a new person, an Exposed-To-Elly. A survivor.

'Isn't she great?' Aideen is asking.

I don't think she's great at all.

'You don't look a size fourteen.'

I don't want to be a size fourteen.

'You're tall. You can get away with it.'

This is the sort of conversation I was dreading. I felt mortified when Elly was checking my waist, the length of my arms from wrist to shoulder. Suddenly I knew how the elephant man felt, surrounded by jeering crowds. It wasn't that anyone laughed but seeing Aideen prancing around in her underwear, unconcerned, confident, made it all a billion times worse.

'I got my book-list this morning.' Well I have to say something to her. We are wandering back to Damien's. I still have no idea what we will be wearing at the wedding. Maybe Rory will get scared and go to his favella all on his own, leaving Sorcha to roam the skies for someone more suitable? Maybe not. I tried crossing my fingers and thinking that if I didn't see the bus to Bishopstown before I counted ten, then everything would work out fine. Guaranteed, the bus trundled past just as I reached eight. Yeutch! It is going to happen. I am going to have to go through with it.

'I couldn't believe how many of the novels I'd already read.' Aideen is shouting above the roar of the stupid double decker that should have been late to fit in with my plans. Great!

'In some ways I'm quite looking forward to next term. Just think, Ness, this time next year it will all be nearly over.'

Wonderful. Sorcha will probably be expecting quins, I will be trying to live down the bridesmaid experience, and Aideen will be laughing all the way to her last two years in school.

'Yeah, I suppose.' Mum isn't here to witness my saying yeah. Anything goes.

Aideen is prattling on. Why am I getting so annoyed? I keep asking myself why, and she keeps talking. She sounds thrilled at the prospect of exams. I am really trying to get excited with her, but frankly, knowing that she's read most of the books leaves me stone cold. Now she's beginning to give me a lecture on the Cork writer Frank O'Connor. I like his stuff. I've read some of it but I can't be bothered to go into that right now. If I open my mouth or unclench my hands I think I might do something that I haven't done for a very long time, hit someone.

'Don't you agree, Nessie?'

I am only half-listening. The other half of me is looking at all the closing-down sales and boarded-up shops. What is wrong with things? A couple of very good-looking Spanish students have passed us by, then turned round and made some comment. They were probably wondering which zoo I'd escaped from, and who my long-haired keeper was.

'Do you think I'm right, Ness?'

Aideen is looking at me oddly. We are passing a surgical supply store. Now that place is gross.

'The more I think about it the more I want to do nursing,' Aideen is announcing.

Maybe I can persuade her to go to Australia or Japan to train. I am thinking evil thoughts about a person I had been so looking forward to being with. I am sick and no, she is not joking, she wants my opinion as to whether I think she'll make a good nurse.

'Do you think I'd have the right attitude?' I don't want this conversation. Suddenly I don't particularly want her walking back with me. A group of girls queuing outside the cinema are shouting out.

'Hi, Aideen. Hi!'

She's receiving a chorus of greetings. How come she knows so many people? Everyone I know knows dozens of other friends. I'll keep on walking and wishing that I hadn't introduced her to Damien and his family. She has enough friends of her own. Why does she have to barge in and borrow mine? I hate being within hearing distance of other folks' popularity ratings.

At every corner someone seems to be asking for money for charities, and then round the next one some poor straggly woman and her even stragglier children are holding out empty margarine tubs, with nothing in the bottom. I can feel my clothes getting tighter by the second. I almost feel little yellow pimples pushing up around my nose, like a flourishing mushroom farm.

'Your legs are longer than I thought,' a breathless

Aideen is shouting behind me.

'My apologies for being an Amazon. Can you think up any more complimentary remarks about my size?' Let me stop! She's looking confused and I think that I am going to scream.

'What do you mean? I think your size is fine.'

'Shut up, Aideen. Don't say any more. You are obviously delighted with the way today is going. I am not.'

'Maybe you're missing your Mum,' she's saying sweetly, looking down at her toes which are poking out of a pair of tiny sandals.

'That's the most ridiculous thing I've ever heard. No doubt you couldn't survive a day without your parents. Well I learnt a long time ago that occasionally you aren't given a choice.' My voice is cracking, and I know that even though I am snarling at Aideen, I am also beginning to cry. But I'm right. I didn't have any say in Dad's departure. Missing Mum? The only thing I'm missing right now is my bedroom, a locked door and a few seconds by myself. Instead we're already at the Kellehers.

'I think we ought to do something this afternoon. What about Quasar?' Aideen is asking awkwardly.

It's a daft idea. It's boiling hot, and Quasar is indoors. It's a good game though, and normally I'd jump at the idea. Seeing as I can't think of anything better, and don't have the energy or the initiative to think up something more exciting, that's where we'll go. I wonder what Mum and Ed are up to? I must check the cat later. God, it's hot! This is my first full day as an eight-week member of the Kelleher household and I'm considering ringing Aunt Fran. Maybe I have sunstroke!

<u>Sixteen</u>

'It's your hormones.'

'I beg your pardon?'

Begging people's pardons is not my scene. I am mutating into my venerable mother. I wish the wedding would disappear, I wish that Aideen would stop calling over, I wish that Damien hadn't been wearing his best silk shirt last week, I wish ...

'Ever since your Mum rang,' Damien continues.

And he took Aideen to the bookshop without me. I know that I was over at my house but he could have waited – Why was he looking so smart!

'Mum said it's your hormones.'

'I hate it when people talk about me.'

'Mum isn't people. Anyway, she said it to Dad.'

'That's ten times worse. I can't stand it when everyone looks at me or starts analysing me.'

'I didn't say that they were analysing you. Dad said is Ness all right. Mum said she thought you might be feeling a bit out of the scene here. Then she said that you were hormonal like Ophelia.'

Great! Ophelia is too young to have hormones; she should be out playing in the puddles. It's raining again. Everything about this life is grot.

'Why don't you ever clear up this dump?'

I'm sitting in Damien's bedroom. I shouldn't be in foul humour but I am. For a start Peter Fairhead called into our house this afternoon. He said it was to remind me that Puss needs booster injections, but I know that's an excuse. He was checking up on me. Mum has rung three times. She's having a wonderful working holiday, says that she's the colour of mahogany and the 'kids' (her word, not mine), are so, and I quote, 'engaging, unlike a lot of students,' unquote. Read into that and fourteen-year-old daughters.

I have been here for eight days and nothing is as I imagined it would be. I have read and re-read that stupid poem from Dad to Mum. I feel homesick. Getting to know the Kelleher clan isn't magic; it's hard work. Damien treats me like another sister. I thought that was what I wanted but now I know it wasn't.

'Talking about hormones, you boys get away scot free.' Damien raises one eyebrow at the 'scot free'. I don't know what it means but I've heard it somewhere. And oh yes, I've found out what a sabbatical is. That's when someone takes a few months', or a few years' break from work ... I think I'll get Mrs Dineen to adopt me. At least she doesn't talk about me like Jo does. Even Jo is different when you are on top of her all the time.

'Ness, will you put the shopping in the cupboard. Ness, stir the gravy, I have to take chewing gum out of Chris's hair. Ness, you bath Cass, she likes you.' This isn't a holiday, it's hard work. And they all go to bed so early.

'What's wrong with this room?' Damien is gazing about what looks like the aftermath of nuclear fall-out and wants to know what's wrong.

'And you're mistaken if you think that boys don't have hormones. They do. How do you think Toby's and my voice broke? Dad didn't thump us with a hammer and hey presto ... deep voices.'

Oh Damien! Why did I think that it would be easy

being here. I am being made to feel a part of the family, but I don't know their ways. Everyone has things to do, whether it's the washing up, cleaning the loos or the landings, peeling carrots or podding peas. The whole thing is worked out on Saturday, after dinner. At home we do what bit needs doing, and the rest seems to take care of itself. Cleaning the landings sounds easy, but as you get down on your hands and knees you almost inevitably prod your knee with a bit of stray lego or the remains of a car. Then, as you're pulling the vacuum through the door the hinge thing at the top swings the door shut and you are left there stranded with half the machine in and the other half out. Toby rescued me this morning. I was standing there, deliberating how to get to the plug, on the other side of the door, when he appeared with it, and the flex and a doorstop.

'Sorry. I guess Mum forgot to tell you how to overcome the trap-door shutting.'

'Did you write to Trass yet?' I asked him as he disappeared to the top floor to play music. There isn't much else to do, seeing as the monsoon seems to have set in for the next forty days and forty nights.

'Yep,' he replied, and then started to whistle cheerily. They all whistle, even Marc.

The weather isn't affecting any of them. All our plans, the swimming in the river, camping in the woods, going to Fota, none of it has happened. Jo says the forecast for July is good. There she was, happy, surrounded by a heap of washing that looked as if it belonged to a bed-and-breakfast. Even the prospect of hanging it in a big shed at the back, where she sticks wet-day washing, didn't seem to bother her. But she told me something interesting. Sophie had been to see a specialist because she is getting more dreamy than

70

usual, and he told Jo after he did a load of tests, that all that was happening was that she was growing up. Poor Ophelia, poor Sophie. Poor Jo, come to think of it. For growing up, read 'getting angry for no reason, hating yourself, and picking on friends'.

'Well, shall I help you to clean your room?'

Grabbing hold of my arm, steering me away from the still warm soldering iron, Damien frog marches me to the door.

'Vanessa Carter, you are being a pain in the rear. Cop yourself on and leave me in peace. I don't want to fight. You do. Go and fight with yourself. Okay?'

He's gone. The door is being locked. What's wrong with me? I'm going to read *The Great Gatsby* by Scott Fitzgerald. That will be one book off my list. If only I were eighteen all this would be behind me. But somewhere in my head I know that I'm the one who's wrong. Tomorrow I will wake up fresh. It's ten thirty. I'll read for an hour in Enda's grisly girly retreat, and I will try hard to be pleasant. I miss you, Mum. I wish I could talk to you, Ed. I think I love you, Damien. Help!

<u>Seventeen</u>

'Morning everyone.'

'Hi Ness. Take a pew. Would you like an omelette or something? All that muesli must get boring.'

'No thanks, Jo. Thanks, Cass.'

Cassie has my bowl ready and a spoon. The phone is ringing in the distance.

'I'll get it.'

Darragh, dressed in cut-down jeans and a black shirt, unbuttoned, leaps away from the table.

'Cool it, little brother.' Damien has to hang onto his glass as Darragh charges past.

'Where did he get that shirt?' Toby wants to know in between mouthfuls of toast.

'Isn't Trass due back today?' Jo asks.

'And Clara.'

I am so happy. The sun is out. Aideen rang. She's coming over to meet up with Clara and Trass. I've got this jealousy thing in hand. It is crazy. So Aideen is better looking than me? So what. I have decided that even if Damien does decide to take her out I will accept it. Things could be a lot worse. At least I'm here, living with the Kellehers. I get the chance to see them all the time. I am going to be more generous. I can do it.

I am going to stop being selfish. I can't wait to see Mum. She's sent me four letters and she's having a great time. She loves the few hours teaching that she's been doing. She says she's bought me a really good present. Not once does she mention Peter. She probably sends him separate letters. Plus I had a letter from Ed. He's in love. Why is he always falling in love? He dropped Tina before he left. He said something really creepy about long-term separation being bad for them both. If you believe that you would believe anything. She and I really got on. Now he has this German woman called Monica. I hope he read his Aids leaflets. I worry about Ed.

'It's for you, Dad.' Darragh, sweeping back his fringe from his face, reseats himself and goes to take a plate.

'Don't touch. That's Nessie's.' Cassie almost breaks Darragh's hand as he pulls a flowery plate towards him.

I have a fan. I've been reading to Cass at night-time. She's quite cuddly and peaceful after her bath. I don't like small kids very much but there is something so fiery about Cassie, you feel you have to keep the flames at bay. She loves all the dopey fairy stories that I used to like. We both cried at the end of 'The Little Match Girl'. I felt a complete twit, particularly as Jo caught me getting tissue for the pair of us.

Marc's back. He looks odd.

'Problems?' Jo wants to know as she hands Darragh and Hugh their sausages.

'Hugh, you sound wheezy. Are you feeling all right?'

Hugh is too busy eating his beans and bangers to answer the question. Marc still isn't saying anything.

'Marc?'

It's that twist in the voice again. Jo is worried.

'Can I have a word with you?' Marc asks as he moves towards the door. He looks awfully pale ... as if something has happened. Not again, not the phone call bit. Not the news delivered and half understood. Not like Dad again ...

'What's up, Ness?' Damien wants to know.

I am sitting very still. I can cope. I can cope. I can ...

'Ness?'

Damien is holding onto me, very close. The girls are looking at me. I know I'm crying. It's just that sometimes when the phone rings it's to tell you something so bad. He doesn't understand. Only Mum and Ed and me. We know what it feels like.

Jo's back.

'Nessie, my love, what's wrong?'

Her voice is so kind, so warm. She's holding me too, and Cass. They're all hugging me.

'It's something bad, isn't it?'

'I'll tell you all about it in a while.'

'It's awful. It reminds me of when Dad ...'

I am sobbing now. Gross. You can keep things under the surface for so long, and then it's like a dam bursting.

'It's nothing to do with any of your family.' Bustling away, Jo gets the boys to clear the table and organises the paddling pool outside, 'Damien, pop Tom into his playpen. Hugh and Darragh, keep an eye on Cass and Chris.'

Chris is hunting around for his water pistol. Everything is normal. But the telephone call means something. You know when things aren't right. Marc hasn't come back.

'Ness? Are you feeling better?'

I nod. I'm feeling a mutt but that's beside the point.

'Right. Now that you're back, Damien, you all have a right to know why I look like Dracula's bride.'

She doesn't. She looks lovely. Her eyes are sad but she looks as if she's full of fight.

'That was a phone call from the office. Your father has been called into a meeting.'

74

Sophie looks scared. Ophelia is impatient to know what's going on. Toby is staring at his feet. Damien is waiting and checking on me every now and then.

'They are shutting down the Cork branch. Dad, along with the rest of them, is being made redundant.'

What a huge, galacious, gigantic relief.

'What does that mean, Mum?' Damien has gone pale too.

I want to shout out, it's fine, Mum is safe, Ed is safe.

'It means that Dad has to find another job.'

That's easy. He's a clever man. He'll get another job.

'He's a bit specialised these days, isn't he, Mum?' Toby asks.

'Yes. That might be a problem. But we're going to have to be brave for Dad's sake. He is very surprised. Nothing at all had been said. They have only just started a brand new project. If he's a bit grumpy tonight, leave him to me. He is very disappointed.'

It's not as if he's died. He'll get another job. Won't he?

Eighteen

The Kelleher house has been like a morgue for the last week. Marc is snappy and eats his meals in another room. I've just returned with Aideen and Hugh has had a really bad asthma attack. We're waiting for the ambulance. He needs Nebucaneserising or something. Nebulising. Jo's just said it. She also hissed at Marc that if he'd been less up-tight, Hugh would be fine. They are fighting. Jo and Marc are fighting. They don't fight. Marc looks as if he's been run over by a truck. I'm going to sit up and wait for them to come back. We were meant to go out tomorrow. I want things normal. I just want things steady.

'Another cup?' Damien is on tea duty. Ophelia is clinging onto the bottom of her nighty. Her toes, her whole body is wrapped up.

'He'll be fine. He's had bad attacks before. He'll be fine.' Toby says it with such conviction you know that he's worried.

'Hugh's like a weather vane. He always has been. If Mum and Dad are upset, he kind of knows it. Mum should have talked to him more about Dad losing his job.' Sophie, dreamy Sophie has put her finger on it. Parents try to protect us instead of sharing what's happening.

'Can I make a cup of coffee? Tea feels kind of weak right now.' Aideen is here in the kitchen, all decked out in matching silky jamies. She's come here to seduce Damien.

'Of course. I'll do it.'

Damien is making coffee, buttering bread. I did Cassie's teeth. I brushed Tom's hair and settled him into his cot. He'll be wandering around tomorrow yelling 'Muuuuum'. He does it every miserable early morning. Why did I invite Aideen back?

Damien is still dressed in his work clothes. We got back from a cake and chocolate session at my house and burst into a huge row. Hugh had let his turtles escape from their tank. They were slopping around in puddles of water and Marc almost trod on one. He began to shout at Hugh. Hugh, all confusion, stood there and began to gasp for breath. Jo gave him his inhaler, and he seemed all right for a little while; then he went blue. I'm scared. I'm afraid. I will not let any one know how I feel. I have to be strong.

'What do they do when they nebulise someone?' Hugh's so little, I need to know.

'It's okay Ness. They give him oxygen. He has had it done before.' Good old Ophelia. I feel grown up, but she knows the answers.

'Listen. We'll be useless in the morning if we stay up all night. Let's settle down and sleep after the tea. Agreed?'

Damien is as upset as the rest of us, but he's been here the longest. He knows what the mornings are like. They start early with Tom, followed by Cass and Chris in hot pursuit. I am not having children. I knew it before; now I know it for definite.

'Thanks, Ness, for the extra pillow. I can't sleep on one.' I'd like to smother Aideen. I want to be here on my own. These are my friends. This is their tragedy and I have Aideen staying, kind of outside it all.

'I brought the sketches. The bridesmaids' dress sketches.'

'I'll look at them tomorrow.' I know I sound brusque. Aideen will assume I'm worried. I am. I am worried. I suddenly hate someone I liked. She seems so twittery all of a sudden.

'Have I done something wrong, Ness?' Her voice is small. Not an Aideen voice at all.

'No. Goodnight,' I answer curtly.

It's useless. I can't sleep. I'm downstairs again and, as ever, my brain is doing somersaults. I have a headache but seeing as I don't know where the medicine box is, I'll let it pound. I don't think that I have been this uneasy for ages. Aideen is slumbering like a baby and I'm here worrying about Hugh. I'm getting cold sitting here in the kitchen. Where are you, Jo and Marc? Why haven't you rung or come back? I'm going to boil the kettle. It's almost daylight outside. I hate this redundancy thing, it's changed everything.

Nineteen

Darragh called out a moment ago. Creeping upstairs without waking everyone is not an easy task. Side-stepping Cassie's plastic bags, Chris's discarded cars and Tom's building bricks must be a bit like avoiding land mines; one false step and the whole house could explode. Darragh shares a room with Hugh. He was worried when he didn't find him on the bottom shelf of their bunk beds. He'd forgotten about the asthma attack. I like Darragh. He tries so hard to be street-wise and cool that you believe most of the time he really is like that. But when I found him, his famous chin-touching fringe sticking up like shark's fins and his trendy extra-large shirt replaced by Batman pyjamas, he just looked like a very frightened little boy. Once I explained that I'd let him know the minute his parents got back he settled down. There's not a whisper from anyone else. I'm too awake to sleep.

Night time programmes are the best. Thank you whoever thought up multi-channel. You get used to being able to flick a switch and on comes what you want. Here the English programmes are re-beamed. They aren't English programmes; they're mainly Australian at five in the morning. Aideen is sound asleep. So is Darragh. I just checked. Everyone else is snoring and Jo and Marc aren't back yet. Yes they are. I can hear the van.

'He's fine, Ness. Isn't he, Marc?'

Jo looks exhausted. So does Marc.

'I'll make you a cuppa.'

79

I feel I have to do something. They are sitting at the big kitchen table holding hands and looking at each other. They look flat out but happy. I feel like doing a cartwheel right across the floor. Maybe everything is going to be fine. Hugh's not going to die. Marc will get a job. Everything will work out. It has to.

'So when can he come home?'

'Tomorrow afternoon, and then we are going out, just as we planned. And Marc is coming too.'

Jo is smiling at him. He has a crinkly face, and the more I look at him the more I realise how much Damien looks like him.

'Hi, is it morning, noon or night?'

It's Aideen. Why does she always have to turn up?

'Sit down and join us.'

Jo is pulling a chair out for her. I'd better get a cup.

'Is he improving?'

Nodding, Jo pours the tea for Aideen and sips at her own quietly.

'I think I'll head for the hills. See you in a while.'

Giving Jo a little kiss, Marc wanders off up to bed. These two people have made it up. I am so glad.

'I think I'll take mine upstairs. Night.'

Aideen rustles off.

Jo's looking at me oddly. I probably made the tea too weak.

'Aren't you and Aideen talking?'

'Of course we are.'

'You could have fooled me. You glared at her as if she was something that Puss had rejected.'

Leave me alone.

'Tell me to stop if you think I am going too far.' Jo is a meddler. I don't want to listen to this.

'I think you are showing classic signs.' That's all

80

right, as long as she think I'm ill.

'Yes, all of the symptoms are there.'

As long as she doesn't make me stay in bed while they all go off out tomorrow.

'The eyes, even down to the chin.'

'What's wrong with my chin?'

Now I'm worried. I've probably developed a rash. I probably am sick ...

'Green, green all the way up.'

'What?' I've gone green?

'You, my young friend, are green with envy. You're jealous, annoyed and put out.'

'I am not.' How dare she. I thought she liked me.

'We have a lot of respect for you, Ness, all of us.' Respect, great. It's let's love a hippo week.

'But you are so closed off and tight. It hasn't been easy for you, all this starting again. Why don't you just come out with it? All the angry stuff. It helps. We do it all the time.'

I've never seen them all getting angry. Apart from this evening, and I was shocked.

'Many's the late night session I've had with Marc, Toby, Damien. Ophelia and Sophie will be joining in soon. That's what families are for; at least that's what my family is about. There's no point in bottling it all up.'

'You'll hate me.'

'I couldn't hate you, Ness. I don't know how.'

And I'm telling her, and she's nodding. She isn't laughing at me. She's listening. She doesn't think I'm a selfish spoilt child. She thinks I am fine.

'You're normal, Ness. Everyone gets jealous. Right now Aideen has it all, but only in your eyes. She doesn't really. She's as angry as you are about what she sees as losing Sorcha. That's natural. She doesn't want to share her. At the moment all the attention is being focussed on a wedding and away from her. That's making her lonely.'

I feel like a hyena. I feel like anything that is low-down and ugly. I feel I ought to go up and apologise.

'As for Damien liking her more than you, he probably does, at the moment.'

Fabulous. I was beginning to feel better, now I feel worse.

'You have been so down and sulky. You have been going round like a rain cloud. Naturally, Damien is going to be with someone who makes him laugh.'

'Have I been that bad?'

She shakes her head from side to side. Now she's really laughing. It's a deep down chuckle.

'No. Worse. You have been a disaster.'

Twenty

Driving in the Kelleher van is a bit like breakfast, disorganised chaos. Now that Hugh has been collected, and he's strapped in along with the rest of us, we can get going. He's fine, in fact he's having a snooze and is resting his head against Cassie, who is being temporarily well behaved and sisterly. She's lodged Batty in his hands. I'd better move it, her, before Hugh wakes up, or there'll be a massive row when he flings her half way back to Cork. Hugh is not a doll person.

'Who organised all these seat belts?' I ask.

'They're good, aren't they? It was Dad, Toby and me. Dad got this magazine about coach crashes. There are so many fatal accidents because passengers get flung about on impact ... hence, seat belts for all.' Damien looks suitably pleased.

It's good the way they can work together. Come to think of it, not one of them has said a word to me about my bad temper. Not Aideen, not anyone. I suspect I would be moaning on and on if the shoe was on the other foot. But I keep remembering what Jo said. Stop thinking the worst about everything and everyone and particularly yourself. I am looking forward to today. We're having our day out.

Aideen is listening to my walkman. I haven't apologised yet. I feel shattered. Two hours' sleep is not enough. But it's good to have Hugh back and safe.

'What's that?'

There's a burnt-out shell of a house, high up on a hill.

'That, Ness, was part of a sorry phase. A lot of the grand houses were owned by the English in the past.'

Here goes, this is when I want to dig a hole for myself and die.

'So during the troubles a lot of them were burnt down. It's a great pity. My grandfather used to tell me about that one. It had a winding staircase and paintings all the way up the walls. The people who owned it farmed and employed a lot of local labour. But some bright spark decided to torch it. No one was killed, but the family left Ireland and the shell is there as a reminder.'

Sometimes I hate history. It can be frightening. It's good to see things from the other side though. If I hadn't come here I wouldn't have ever considered why there is so much bitterness about England. But it's difficult when you hear it. I would love it if one day my friends came back with me to some of the places that I know well. That can make me sad at times. They all know where they are going. They recognise the names of the little areas and the bridges and the old churches. I know hardly anything about anywhere. I know a few street names, but that's in the centre of Cork.

'Where are we going?'

'You are going to love this name, Ness. Kilbrittain.' Everyone is laughing, and I am too. These are my friends. And Kilbrittain is a sea-side place, that's all. Kil means church; it's an old Irish word, and the Brittain bit was probably someone's name, pronounced Brithain. Only words, with a different meaning.

Aideen and I are sitting together on the beach, and the subject of Elly's sketches comes up. I had looked at them before we left the house. I can't keep on calling Elly Eleanora because her drawings, sketches, were so good. Thinking back to that day at the hotel, all she was was different. But the outfits are something that I could not see myself in. They are not 'ballet docs,' and they are definitely not as appalling as I thought they could be. What are they?

I'm going to shock my mother. She'll be there all ostrich feathers and silk and glamour, and I am going to make her sit up and take notice.

'I think those sketches are great,' I say. 'We'll be fine for the wedding.'

Suddenly Aideen erupts like a volcano that had been waiting for centuries to explode.

'I don't give a flying monkey about the wedding. What's happening, Ness? I can't keep quiet forever. I can't be the well brought up little girl who let's folk walk all over her. What have I done? I really love you. You are my friend, probably one of the very few I'd dare bare my soul to. You're treating me like ...'

'Aideen, I don't know how to say it.'

I was tired, sitting there on the beach. It seemed to take hours to unload the car. I was tired anyway after Hugh's experience the night before. We'd eaten sandwiches. Jo had made all sorts of veggie treats for me. I don't know when, but she had. Mushroom pâté. How do you make mushroom pâté on no sleep and a husband who is being made redundant?

You cannot come out with it, directly. 'I have gone through a patch of hating you.' Saying that would be terrible. I tried all sorts of mumbled explanations, Aideen sat listening, pulling a towel over her knees and fiddling with sand. The beach was beautiful, and although there were plenty of other families around,

Marc had found us an isolated spot. He and Jo were walking, Hugh and Darragh were tearing around on the sand playing football. Ophelia and Sophie were exploring the rock pools with Cass and Chris. Toby and Damien were far away, swimming, and Tom had done the right thing – he was sleeping in his pushchair. Don't ever take a pushchair to a beach. Pushing it through the sand is a bit like moving a bull dozer. I have learnt a lot over this holiday ...

'How did I do it?' Aideen asked. 'How did I change to make you hate me so much?'

She thought that it was her fault.

'You didn't. I did, I can't tell when; it crept up on me.'

I still didn't know how to mention about her and Damien. Aideen knows I like him, but being around him all the time at their house has made me like him so much more.

'I'm jealous.' I said it. Saying those words was like chewing on a ton of sand. I am jealous, and I felt as if I was saying I'm a murderess, I am a thief. I am ... any of a thousand things I don't want to be. Talk about humiliating. I felt sick and quivery inside.

'Jealous!' Aideen yelled at me. 'Of what?'

Tom began to toss around in his sleep. Hugh and Darragh were looking over at the pair of us. Even the crashing about of the sea seemed to have temporarily quietened. I had a feeling that everyone, even the huge rook who was tottering around beside us seemed to have turned his cheeky beak on our conversation.

'You always seem so happy, even over Sorcha, you're coping. Then ...' Oh but this is going to be the hard bit.

'Damien likes you ...' There, I said it. Aideen can work out the rest.

'So?'

'Aideen, please ...' She was still looking bemused.

'And I thought that you were angry with me because of Ed.'

'Ed?' My turn for confusion.

'You must have guessed.'

Aideen had been adoring Ed from the sidelines ever since she had met him. I told her in no uncertain terms that Ed was a hopeless case. He loves being in love every five minutes. He's always swapping and changing. It would break Aideen's heart to have anything to do with him. And he is way too old.

'I know,' she said hopelessly.

Working it out was far less terrible than I thought it would be. No, I cannot see Aideen and Ed together, but if she wants to wait around for him, that's fine. As for Damien and me, Aideen said that it was obvious that he likes me. I know that ... She also said something that was so good.

'Being friends, close friends is sometimes going to be like this, I suppose. You end up knowing someone so well you treat them badly. Please Ness, next time, can we try and talk about it before it ends up like this? You have this look. It's as if you know that you are better than everyone else. And your accent, that doesn't help either. It can take on this very grown-up high and mighty tone. I don't know how you do it. But you are frightening when it happens.'

So, as I hang onto Cassie's damp little paw walking the length of the beach, I am trying, and it's difficult, to soften up. I can't help my face and my voice, can I? Maybe I can.

Twenty-one

We're getting started on our project today. Making shape of the terraced houses behind the university, where Trass lives.

'Dad.' Damien has a certain sound when he wants something. It's not wheedling or horrible, but you can hear the question before the question.

'You know those cans of paint in the big shed?'

'Yeeees.'

You can tell that Marc knows what's coming next.

'May we take a few? We thought we'd get started on the third house. Seeing as we have loads of colours ...'

'With pleasure, but check with Frank Coyne before you get started. He mightn't like our choice of potent pink and luscious lavender that we went in for when we were first married.'

Potent pink? Luscious Lavender? It sounds as if they went through a massage parlour phase. They probably did! Frank Coyne is the councillor that Jo knows. He's nice enough but very cautious, the sort who would think for ten minutes before saying anything that might incriminate him.

All the Kelleher sheds and outhouses have different names. Big medium and small only cover the first three. There's also the blue one. Cassie was responsible for that. She was supposed to be in her cot having an afternoon sleep. She wasn't. She was decorating the shed blue. Then there's the chicken one. For a while Jo kept chickens.

'Not to eat,' I wailed.

'No. For their eggs, dopey.'

I couldn't imagine them wringing chickens' necks. Anyway, the chickens decided they didn't like laying eggs and rats decided they liked all the grain that was left out for the chickens. So ... the chicken shed is full of old bikes. Toby ran a bike repair business last summer. I wish I'd known them all then. I was still settling in. Come to think of it, if someone had said the word rat to me last year, I would have died a thousand deaths. Now I am kind of accepting this half-country, half-city existence. A lot of people in England have totally the wrong impression about Ireland. It's down to lack of information and snobbery. Someone like Dad could see through the bigoted bits. He would have loved it here, if only he'd given himself the chance.

It's July the fourteenth. Damien has organised a wheelbarrow which is now overloaded with paint, brushes, turpentine, old rags and Cassie and Chris. Jo and Marc are going to Waterford. Maybe it's even rainier there than here. If I had my way I would rename Cork, Waterlogged! They have the baby with them and Hugh and Darragh have scattered off to friends' houses. Ophelia is going somewhere too, so I suppose Sophie is tagging along with her. We have the twins anyway.

'I want Ness to push.' Cassie is still heavily into adoring me. I thought that she might enjoy *The Lion the Witch and the Wardrobe*. We read a bit each night. She wants to be my blood sister. I told her it wasn't healthy. I'm sure that some night she'll prod me with a needle. This is a very pushy human being. How can such a bonded family produce a creature so unlike themselves? I don't know. HIV stands for heavily into a vegetarian, in Cassie's case.

'Ness, do you have the milk?' Yes I do. Toby has to remember the coffee, Damien the sugar and Cassie and Chris are sharing tea bags and spoons. All very democratic. I raised the roof when Toby informed me I was on tea-duty.

'Why?' I asked.

'Because you're good at it.' He replied.

'So are all of you,' I retorted.

'Ness, I'm winding you up. If you do it today, me tomorrow, Damien the day after ...'

I feel very strongly about sharing duties. But then Toby knew that. Why do people find me so easy to tease? I don't know. But I do feel happy right now. I'm looking forward to some good cleaning up, some great painting, lots of action in the terraced houses. Things are happening, at last.

Twenty-two

'What is that?'

Damien has found a bunch of papers behind a shelf in one of the cupboards. He would call it a press. I am still into identity. It's a cupboard.

'Don't know', says Trass. 'Mum and I haven't begun to clear out half the stuff that was left behind in our home.'

We are standing in house number three. It is more of a disaster area than Damien's bedroom.

Opening up the dusty bundle tied with ribbon, Clara and I, head to head, begin to read the letters. They are love letters and I feel embarrassed looking at them.

'Shall we put them away for now?' I ask.

'Yes. Whoever Kit Fitzpatrick was he certainly knew how to pen a letter,' says Clara, folding them back into a roll and putting them to one side. The little I'd read reminded me of the card that Dad had sent Mum. The envelopes were addressed to Rebecca Stein and the letters signed Kit. One day, maybe, I'll write a story around them. I'm glad that Clara felt the same way. We were trespassing and knew it. Once upon a time in Cork there was a large Jewish community. Rebecca was a part of it. This is such a little place with so much history. This tiny, unmade-up house holds a sad love story. Awesome.

The houses were owned by old people who have been dead for ages, and so the whole group of six have been bought up by the council. To get to them you have to climb ancient steps. Getting the wheelbarrow up was not easy.

Everywhere in number three is filthy, but according to the architect and surveyor the house is structurally sound. You could have fooled me. The walls are mildewed and the floors uneven.

'Where's the kitchen?' I have been looking for the last ten minutes for a place to plug in the kettle. As I am tea person I am treating the role with suitable efficiency.

'This is it, Ness.' Trass is waving her arms about the little room that we are standing in.

'But ...' This cannot be a kitchen. This is a space, an area. There is an ancient ceramic sink which you could bath a small horse in. There are taps that don't work. Where are the power points?

'Nessie, you are looking shocked. What's the matter?'

The matter should be obvious to anyone but a moron. The electric points are round; the wiring is exposed. This place is decades out of date.

Damien's face screws up as he remembers something. 'I should have thought of that. Dad mentioned it the other day. He's coming over with a few friends to start on the rewiring. Sorry folks, but you'll be relieved, Ness. No water, no electricity. I got so carried away when I knew that Mum and Dad were going out for the day. I wanted to surprise them and Councillor Coyne.'

He is looking pleadingly at me.

'Could you and Toby go and get cokes or something?'

'Not Toby. Me. I want to go with Nessie,' Cassie is wailing. To think I was jealous of Aideen's popularity! Being unpopular would be a lot easier. Save me from Cassie's adoration.

'Or we can go to my house. Mum won't mind,' Trass

92

suggests.

'Look at the state of us,' Damien is pointing to Cassie, happy again and digging in amongst a pile of wood shavings. Meanwhile Chris is writing letters in the dirt of a half open window.

'I think your Mum can do without any more hassle than she already has,' says Damien.

'Great, no water, no power. What are we doing here until there is water and power?' Because they are always there, the basics, you tend to forget that not everyone has the same facilities. Suddenly operation clear-up looks doomed.

'All we need do today is sweep around a bit. Have a look and see what needs doing. I'll make a list. Who has a pencil or something?' Damien is now looking expectantly at me. This is going to be a groupy head-shaking session.

No pencil, no paper, so Cassie and I are marching to the shop, which feels as if it's a hundred miles away because Cass walks so slowly and has to stop and inspect every feather, stone and interesting anything that she comes across.

At last, the shop. Wait a moment. A very large moment. This place looks closed. Pushing against the door, Cassie and I almost catapult into the dark little recess that leads into a tiny corridor where there is a counter, and a person sitting on a stool looking warily at us. I think it's a person, but it could be a dummy. The light from the outside is only just getting in.

'Do you have any cokes?' I say into thin air.

'No.' The dummy speaks.

'Some writing paper and a pencil?' I want to get out of here fast. This dimly-lit person isn't exactly jumping for joy that Cassie and I are here to shop. It said Siopa outside; that means shop. There was a kind of window with yellow paper against it; at some point in time there must have been something in the window that needed protecting from the sun.

'No.'

'Thank you.' I'm getting out. I've gone a few steps before I realise Cass isn't with me.

'Cassie.' I sound nervous, I can hear my voice clearly.

'Cass. Come here now.' Silence. I can hear breathing. I really needed this. My day would have been incomplete without the no water, no electricity and now no Cassie.

I look up and down the street. There is no sign of her. I feel ill. I have lost a four-year-old minx. She has been stolen. She is on her way to some den of ...

I run back to the shop, frantic now. There she is!

'Thank you, Mrs Carberry. Ness, look what Mrs Carberry gave me.' Cass, with a handful of jellies, is standing beside me.

'Where were you? What are those?' A bit roughly, judging by the look in Cassie's eyes, I take hold of her hand to make sure that they are sweets and not something more sinister. You can't be too careful. We're outside the shop at this stage.

'She said that we could go and see her cats. Shall we go and see them? I told her that you liked cats so I said I'd find you first.'

Oh Cassandra Kelleher, have you no fear? Children feel too safe some of the time. They don't think about all the bad things that could happen, because more often than not the bad things don't happen. Well, they do where I come from. Ed and I were never out of Mum's sight. Her paranoia meant that the pair of us

94

were too terrified until we were about twelve to even ask directions from a stranger. And now here's Cass, plus jellies which she shouldn't have accepted and we're going to see some old crone's cats.

'I think we ought to go back to the others. Come on. We'll see the cats some other day.' Taking hold of Cass I try to move her but she is rooted to the spot.

'Won't,' she bawls.

People are watching me as I attempt to pull her. She weighs a ton when she chooses. Bending down to pick her up, I know that we should get away. She gives me a slap on the side of my head. I feel like battering her. I won't, but I am only centimetres away from practising corporal punishment.

'Say you're sorry,' I demand.

'Can we see the cats?' is her reply.

My ear is stinging. She ought to become a featherweight boxer. I always suspected that Chris, her twin, was a bit of a wimp running away from her on a fighting day. Now I know why he runs.

'Two minutes, that's all. Understood?'

I have given in to a four-year-old. I am a bruised and broken Vanessa and it took this diminutive fiend to do it. I knew I didn't like small kids for a reason.

Twenty-three

Walking back into the shop I notice that Mrs Carberry, as Cass called her, has disappeared from behind the counter. Cass strides ahead and pushing back a curtain we are in a tiny sunlit sitting room. And there, on a chair, a side board, the television, the settee, in fact everywhere I look there are assorted cats, kittens and a minuscule yorkshire terrier. The smell is indescribable. It was odd in the shop bit, musty, old, but in here it is overpowering. These are not house-trained pets. Puss is probably a relative. Cassie is oblivious; she's stroking one, then the next. As she gets over to the dog, I shriek, 'Don't.' Too late, Cassie has him in her arms and is showering him with kisses.

'Cassie, put him down. He might have bitten you.' Apart from biting her, he looks as if he's a walking rabies carrier. His coat is long and tangled and he really smells.

'He likes children.'

Turning round to see who has half-reassured me that the creature is safe to hold, I see Mrs Carberry. I can't help myself, I am staring. She is tiny. She has little wispy bits of white hair, and her face is wrinkled and shrivelled.

'Can I go outside, Mrs Carberry?' Cassie is asking. She should be terrified. This old lady looks like the living dead.

'You can of course.' Shuffling to a door the old lady opens it onto a tiny yard, where about five more cats are basking in the sun, in amongst weeds and boxes and rubbish.

I don't know what to do. I don't think that we should be here. Cass doesn't sense danger. I do. There is something terribly wrong about all this. I've never met Mrs Dineen's ninety-four year old mother, but I suspect that Mrs Carberry is probably her grandmother.

'She said you like cats.'

Oh no! It's conversation time. Her accent is terribly well-off, a sort of dowager duchess voice. It doesn't fit her body at all.

'I do.' I think I do, well, one at a time I like them.

'They throw them out when they get big. People, they chuck their pets out like rubbish.'

She's pottering about and suddenly, like a tidal wave, the whole lot begin to move off their various resting places. Finding a tin opener she begins to open a tin. Her old hands are a mixture of white and blue; all the veins seem to have popped onto the top and her fingers are curved, the nails too long. I'm disgusted. I don't want to be this close to old age.

'Here, let me do that.'

Going over to where the poor old thing is almost submerged by heaving fur and yapping flesh, I take the lid off the tin. As I'm doing it, one of the smaller cats begins to climb up my bare leg.

'Yeowww. Get him off!' Now another is clawing its way up my thigh. Mrs Carberry is clicking away at them, explaining soothingly that I'm a nice visitor, a friend of the little girl. Talking of little girls, where is the little monster?

There are eighteen saucers in the cracked sink. There is an old tin kettle that looks like the one the jolly swagman threw out after waltzing with Matilda. There are bags and more bags of I don't know what.

'Do you have anyone to help you?' I ask. I have been given a cup of milk. I hate warm milk, but there is no fridge, and she's so sweet in a macabre kind of way. After she's persuaded the cats that I wasn't their latest scratch post, she ushered a few of them outside to join Cass, who is contentedly playing with a snow-white kitten. I didn't understand at first why it is part of this menagerie, until Cass explained, solemnly, 'It's her eyes.'

I looked more closely. The poor little thing is blind; she has a white film where the coloured bit should be. Horror movie time again. Half of these animals should be put down.

'I don't need help. I need no body and no body needs me,' Mrs Carberry told me angrily.

'Who does your shopping?'

I was going to ask her if anyone helps her with the housework, but that would be a pointless question, because there hasn't been too much housework done in this place since the 'fifties.

'I do. My son, when he was here, he did it. But ...'

She is trying to sit on one of the chairs; cats squirm away and then resettle on top of her.

'After my son died I let the business run down. I get to the shops all right.'

The nearest supermarket is about ten minutes' walk away. How does someone as old as that do shopping?

Cassie rushes in, the little white kitten tucked under her chin, half on her shoulder like a parrot.

'Can we come back every day? I'll tell Mum. She'll love Emma.'

Emma, who is Emma?

'Can I call the kitten Emma, please, Mrs Carberry?'

'You come back any time you choose, little girl, and you can bring your big sister with you. She helped feed my cats.'

Me, Cassie's big sister. I would rather be accused of never missing *Neighbours* but I don't think that Mrs Carberry would appreciate the sacrifice.

Judging by my legs which are covered in scratch marks, these are vampire cats. I am going to have to do something about Mrs Carberry. What she is living in is squalor. I like mess, good old-fashioned chaos. But I don't like dirt. The very thought of going back there makes me feel ill. But to think that she is there all on her own except for her animal friends (and they aren't too friendly), makes me feel worse. Why couldn't Cassie have found an ordinary shop? Life would have been so much easier!

After we left Mrs Carberry and returned to the others at number three I felt terrible. Yes, part of it was that I stank; so did Cass. Part of it was that my legs, hands and body hurt, from the scratches. But the other bit was that she looked very sad as we left, and made us promise to come back tomorrow.

'How about it?' I asked the others.

'Would she mind if we all turned up and offered to clean up?' Trass wanted to know.

'She's very nice,' Cass was telling Chris. 'And she's my old lady, not yours,' she said, reinforcing the *my* with a hefty thump.

I can't stand the thought of her there in that poky little place. She showed us all of the rooms. The shop is built into the hallway. She and her husband ran it. They only ever had one son. He was, as she put it, one of God's children. I thought she meant a kind of saintly person. Mr Carberry has been dead for twenty years and her son for five. She said that she was eighty-three. If she'd told me she was a thousand I wouldn't have been surprised.

There is the little cat parlour and a back kitchen; a scullery I suppose. The toilet is outside. How does she manage in the winter? This is primitive. Cass and I went upstairs on our own. She doesn't go upstairs any more.

'I might fall, and there's no one to catch me. Not that I need catching.'

Up there were two bedrooms. Mice had eaten away at the bedspreads and the papers that were covering the furniture. There were droppings everywhere. The cats are a real help. They probably stand in the shop doorway and invite in the local rodent population. Then when Mrs Carberry forgets to feed them they probably stroll upstairs and catch dinner.

There weren't any bulbs in the lights. I asked her why.

'Can't reach. I have my torch and I have my fire and my lamp by my bed.'

And then it struck me. Where did she sleep? There was no sign of a bed downstairs. She showed me. In a corner, under a cat or three was a chest. It was beautifully carved and looked terribly old. I am not a furniture person but this was a beautiful oak box. After we'd shifted the cats she opened the lid, and there inside was a duvet, without a cover, and a pillow. Her son William had bought the duvet for her. She was very proud of it.

'My father made the chest. He was at sea, ship's carpenter. When he was home he would make furniture for my mother.'

And she began to remember back. How could she ever have been my age? It isn't possible that she was once young. But it was, because she got out an old chocolate box which was full of photographs. She showed us Mr Carberry. He was tall, dark and handsome. It is so sad that they didn't all die together. But she's full of fight. Then she showed us her wedding photograph. I stopped. I couldn't believe it. There were these two young people. She had doe eyes, dark dark hair, and a soft veil caught just above her forehead in a floral band. The dress she was wearing was high at the neck and flowed down to a hem that whirled out.

'Silk. Father gave it to mother as a gift. He brought it back from China. She kept it for me. She made my dress, then I made William's christening robes from it. I still have it.'

'Do you have any photographs of William?' I wanted to know.

'There.' She handed me a picture of a small boy. He looked ordinary, not in any way different.

Cass was beginning to grow impatient, having explored the house, ascertained that the jelly store was empty, replaced the little white cat back in the yard. She was ready for more adventure.

'We'll be back tomorrow,' she called out as she pushed back the curtain and ran for the front door. Yes, we most definitely will. Tomorrow I'm going to introduce Mrs Carberry to my friends.

Twenty-four

In two days time Ed will be back. That means that I have only two more days at the Kellehers. It's been a strange old summer. The weather has been atrocious with odd splashes of sunshine yellow in between. I've learnt a tiny bit of patience, a dollop of humility and an overdose of humanity. I don't mean that horribly. I mean that being with so many different people, all those different ages, has made me think. I hope Cassie will be all right. She and I make a curious couple, but I actually enjoy her meddling company. At least she hasn't dug a knife into my arm, guaranteeing blood sisterhood!

I called in to see Mrs Dineen this morning. She informed me that the two cats are getting along beautifully. I know, I know, it's not sensible, but I had to do it. After we went back, and Mrs Carberry accepted our offer of help, I was haunted by the sight of Cassie's Emma, the white kitten. She is a dear little thing (the kitten, not Cassie). She had cataracts. I thought the vet was joking but, after her operation, her eyes are beginning to heal. Emma and Puss disappear through the cat flap together. He prowls around and casually returns a couple of hours later, but she pops back fairly quickly. I don't know what Mum will say. I'm not sure that she is going to be too pleased about a second resident cat. But it had to be done. And in the end it was Peter who helped out. Yes, that Peter, the vet whom I thought I hated.

A couple of days after we began to sort out some of the mess at Mrs Carberry's, Damien, very gently, suggested it might be easier if she had just one cat and one dog. Now Mrs Carberry can either be altogether charming, or extremely vindictive and angry. The only one of us she likes without question is Cassie. They make a fine pair. They are both unpredictable.

'And where, pray, are you going to take the poor things? Down the road you'll say to me, but you mean something else.'

She has icy blue eyes, which, when she's not in the middle of a tirade, look normal; when she's roused they are like steel.

Damien explained that we would find homes for them. He begged Clara to take one.

'A cat. A cat at our house. Damien, it's a great idea. Now feed it to my mother.'

Clara's mother is a difficult woman. She is a bit of a local social. That means she is involved in lots of things where she can be seen. She has a totally paw-free house and I think she fully intends to keep it that way. She treats Trass like a stray animal. I dread to think what she would do with a proper stray.

'Aideen, what about you?'

Damien was trying to do all this quietly, so that Mrs Carberry wouldn't be upset. She appeared to be watching racing on the television. We've made her a permanent bed downstairs. None of it has been easy. Any help she regards as interference. During the first session of pulling the yellow cellophane paper from the front shop window, and clearing up the hall and near the counter, I took her duvet to be cleaned. She objected, but Cass calmed her down by offering to sit on her knee and listen to stories. I don't know how

Cassie does it. I want to help, but I couldn't get as physically close to old Mrs Carberry as Cassie does. After getting the duvet cleaned it seemed a waste of money not to get a few covers for it. Thank you, Mum, for the money. I didn't know what to do with so much. Now I know.

Marc and Jo and Marie McDermot have also become a part of the big Carberry clean up. Marc and some of his friends are building her a shower and a loo off the scullery. She was furious but unwillingly accepted that it might make sense during the winter. Apparently the social services wanted to put her in a home. Naturally she refused. As long as we keep an eye on her, they seem to think that, for now, it will be all right. Isn't it terrible that, because you are old and alone, somebody might be able to take you away from where you live?

'Well, Aideen, one cat, just one?' Damien pleaded.

'Damien, a wedding is enough to turn my mother's hair grey; a cat would send her scurrying into insanity.'

'Don't people like cats in this country?' I asked.

'I have a feeling that we are not quite as sentimental about animals as you seem to be over the water. Cats are for killing rats and mice. Dogs are for herding sheep and guarding houses,' Clara hissed in reply.

'Well, all this wearing of rubber gloves, shovelling filth and cleaning floors will be a total waste of time and energy unless we get rid of some of these creatures,' Damien whispered.

'Getting rid of them, is it now? You youngsters are all the same. They have rights, they deserve homes,' Mrs Carberry snapped at us.

I felt like reminding her that we had tried our hardest to help her, to make life more comfortable. But I knew if I mentioned any of that we would be promptly shown the door. And despite her ill-humour and her complaints, I like her. Then I remembered Peter Fairhead. My opinion of Peter has been consistently negative. He seems to like me and I loathe him in return. I don't like it when I see Mum going out with him. He looks too old, he acts too friendly, he doesn't fit in. Ed disagrees, but he's going through an 'I-am-a-mature-male, soon-to-leave-school phase,' so I ignore him. But, Peter is a vet.

'I've had an idea,' I said out loud.

Twenty-five

'Ness, lovely to see you. Greetings, Vanessa's compatriots.' Vanessa's compatriots! Peter can still sound creepy. Maybe he isn't sure how to talk to us.

'Where's Puss? There's a lot of feline enteritis around.'

'Peter, I am not here about Puss. I'll do that next week.'

Frowning he led us past the surgery bit and into his sitting room. It's a cosy place; he has two spaniels called Jekyll and Hyde. Clara says that it makes sense. She thinks he's a bit odd too. The dogs are twins, and, a bit like Cass and Chris, totally unalike. Jekyll is the male. He's boisterous to the point of being dangerous, and Hyde, better known as Heidi, is a subservient female who crawls around looking for attention. I would like to give her assertiveness training but the very second that she spots me she disappears behind one of Peter's squashy chairs, with her stumpy tail stuck between her legs. I think it's cruel to dock a dog's tail. Peter says it isn't.

'How's your lovely mother?' What an opening line.

'Fine. Peter, we have got to know an old lady, near the development project place.'

'The terraces? Yes I know it.'

'She has hundreds of cats.'

'Old Mrs Carberry. She used to be an actress. Did you know that?'

Our Mrs Carberry? On the stage?

'No, I didn't know that, but we are trying to help out

106

clearing up the house.'

'She could very well shoot you for that. She's a strange old bird.'

As he stood there, a glass of what looked like sherry in one hand and the other dragging at Jekyll's ears to keep him down, he looked almost human.

'We need to get rid of some of her pets.'

Frowning, he said a fierce 'sit' to Jekyll who hopped onto a chair. Heidi whimpered from behind her hiding place.

'Well?'

'Give me a while and I'll call a few people. How many are there, roughly? Some of them wander in and out but they aren't the real problem. It's her regulars that need good homes I suppose.'

'Thirty,' Toby replied emphatically.

'There is one, a Persian, that she loves the most.'

It's an arrogant bluey grey affair, all bushed out and superior. I suspect that he got lost rather than ditched, because he has the good manners to go outside once in a while. I must introduce him to Puss. That Persian has class!

Peter disappeared for about twenty minutes. I had a good look at all the photographs he had on his piano. He must spend hours dusting them. Some of them were browny tints, his parents probably. Some were colour photographs. He looked old even when he was young. Poor Peter.

'Any luck?' I had adopted the role of spokesperson. Trass and Toby were looking at ancient editions of *Country Life*, which they hastily put down when he came in. Clara was talking soothingly to the personality-less Heidi, and Damien and Jekyll were wrestling on the rug.

'Sit.'

Miraculously Jekyll sat. It was Damien who said it. Peter looked confused.

'Mmm, lots. How did you do that?' he asked Damien. Damien shrugged.

'Right. There are good homes for eight kittens. There are possible farm jobs for twelve adult cats. There is an old people's home which will accept either one cat or a kitten, no more. Vanessa, are some of these animals very old? Possibly one or two are beyond help.'

I knew what he was asking. Euphemism is euthanasia in this case.

'No way, Peter. There is no way that I can tell her a lie. Either the cats go to a good home, or they stay.'

The room was silent. Toby and Trass looked sweet, occasionally smiling at each other. Lucky Trass. Clara had persuaded Heidi out from behind the chair and was gently stroking her.

'How many are left?'

We reached an estimate of around ten, including the white kitten.

'I'll take Emma. That's the blind one.'

'Is that wise, Ness, given that it took a degree of persuasion to allow the famous Puss under your roof?' He said it with such twinkly merriment that I was taken aback.

'Wise or not, I think that I can get round Mum. She'll be so happy to see Ed and me ...'

'I get the picture.' He suddenly seemed to relax.

'Ten?' Rubbing his chin he began to walk around the room. Jekyll, quite relaxed, was lying against Damien's leg. Lucky Jekyll!

'I wonder!'

And with that he was gone.

It all felt hopeless. Mrs Carberry's house would be manageable with one tiny dog and one house-trained cat; otherwise all our efforts of clearing away the filth would be wasted. You needed rubber gloves to work around there. Do I have to say more? And yet I know why she wanted to do something for the strays. She has a good heart and poor eye sight. Half the time she doesn't see what her pets are up to.

Peter walked back in with a cheery smile on his face and a plate of biscuits which Jekyll almost snatched from him.

'I have some splendid news.'

We all waited. Heidi was glued to Clara's side. Maybe Clara will take over the assertiveness training, and Damien the obedience classes.

'All catered for. I asked a few generous patients if they would consider one more pet. When I mentioned Mrs Carberry they were all more than willing to offer. She was a very popular woman before all the tragedies.'

'Tragedies?' Trass questioned with her soft voice, her big eyes getting wider.

'If you were to mention the name Barton to your parents,' Peter explained, looking from Toby to Damien and Clara, 'then they would remember. She was known as Dorothy Barton. She and her husband were terribly well known on the stage, until he contracted multiple sclerosis. She left the theatre, and quietly disappeared from the bright lights, just supported herself and William with the shop. My mother, God rest her soul, knew her. Dorothy didn't have friends; she was used to contacts. Anyway, she explained to my mother that once, during a tour of the South of England, she bought excellent wine in a small vintners called Carberry's; so for privacy, she adopted that name.'

'And William?'

'He was a wonderful son and a great source of joy to them both, until some idiot drunk driver knocked him down in his first year at UCC. He was doing medicine.'

Peter looked terribly angry, and I just wanted to run away.

'He survived, but his brain was badly impaired. Anyway, Ness, your kitten mission is complete.'

We walked home silently. Sometimes there isn't anything that you can say. Suddenly I understood what she meant by 'one of God's children'.

Twenty-six

I am jumping, I am skipping. I haven't seen Ed for nearly two months. I have missed him. I have been irritated by his lack of letters but I suppose writing in a tent isn't the easiest option. Jo is only just hanging onto Tom, who has suddenly developed Cass's latent characteristics of being ultra hyper-active. Where did that calm baby disappear to? Heaven knows.

Mum rang last night. I really wanted to talk to her. I didn't mention Emma. I know how much she disapproves of those who travel on four legs. She is taking some time off to visit Colorado. I must look up how far she's travelling. Do they have a lot of air crashes in the States? Mrs Dineen is here. She's brought Mum's car to the airport, so that Ed can drive us home. I am even wearing a skirt. Jo gave it to me. I think that I look like a hippy. My permed hair is growing long. It is actually growing in the promised ringlets it was meant to do about a year ago. I feel so pleased. I feel grown up. I can't wait to get back to my own room. I love the Kellehers but suddenly I need a lot of peace and quiet. There is a distinct lack of precious silence there.

Tonight I'm going to sit up talking to Ed until it gets light outside. Mrs Dineen has prepared a big supper; there's turkey and ham for Ed and there are about ten salads for me. Then tomorrow I'm going to introduce him to Mrs Carberry. It's going to be so good ...

Jo and Marc knew all about the Bartons through their parents. They had actually heard of them. It could only happen here: three million people and a famous couple disappeared and reappeared as Mr and Mrs Carberry and son. I like it in one way. In another it's kind of sad. They were a famous couple who shunned the cinema and worked in small and grand theatres all over the world. They had been to places like India and Africa long before other stage schools were set up there. Trying to visualise crotchety Mrs Carberry as the beautiful woman in the bridal gown still doesn't work, but it does make us all try to understand her more. We won't mention that we know, not unless she says something. It isn't that I like secrets. I hate them. I need everything up front. Otherwise my jealousy bug might take root again. But I think I understand. It's back to Ireland being very intimate, everyone knowing everyone else. Mrs Carberry has earned her privacy. One day will someone look at a picture of Sorcha's wedding, with Aideen and me as bridesmaids, and wonder who we were? That makes me shudder. Stop thinking, Ms Carter. We're here at the airport. Any second now Ed will be back.

'Ness.' It's Damien, looking serious considering that this is a happy day. He came to join us at the airport.

'You look ...'

He's stopped. All I want him to say is that I look right, a number one sister for a number one brother.

'Dumb word. You'll think I'm a creep, but you look good.' Thanks, Damien. Good is how I feel. I can't believe the time has gone by. I'm almost looking forward to the wedding in a sadistic kind of way. Well the 'it' can't be nearly as bad as thinking about it, can it? Damien has made a big effort. He looks good too. He's wearing his Mr Giant Jeans or whatever they're called, a new shirt ... Who gave him a grey shirt? Jo probably. I keep getting this urge to fling my arms round him, to say how much I am ...

Come on, Vanessa. What are you? You are a fourteen-year-old spotty kid who happens to have got a few things together. I am so grateful for all the help that I've been given over the last few busy weeks. Thank you, Peter. Thank you, Marc. Right now I love everyone.

'It's down. The plane is down.'

Mrs Dineen is hopping around on one foot. She is delighted beyond measure.

'There he is,' she states emphatically. If that's my brother he looks as if he's been working for MI5 undercover.

'No, it's not. Is it?'

This very tall man-looking person has got off the plane. Ed left Ireland with a regulation school haircut; now it's long and curly. I've never seen Ed with long hair. He's tanned and his jeans are almost hanging off him.

I feel as if my face is frozen into a grin. I am smiling at everyone and they are smiling back. Damien is frog-marching Chris to the toilet with Cassie howling after him because they're walking so fast. Why do little kids spend their lives looking for toilets? I think I've seen the insides of more public conveniences since living with the twins than I thought was possible. Cassie and Chris dive into bars, restaurants, hotels. It's no bother to them. Once they need to go, that's it, the rest of living stops dead until they are satisfied.

I can see him. Oh Ed, I wish Mum were here too.

The weather has remembered that it's July. I am tempted to remind it that in just over a week it's

August and I will be left with hardly any more freedom time. Incredible. But it's brilliant having Ed at home again.

He makes things feel safe, normal. His decision to do all his return-from-Germany washing has not been a success. He's busily bleaching jeans that should be pale blue, back to pale blue. Washing them with a red rugby shirt was not a clever idea. It must run in the family ... do you get it? Run, dye ... Never mind. I was looking forward to having him back, but I didn't know how much. We are non-stop talkers when the mood takes us, but catching up on his news from abroad was amazing, and frightening.

The group that he went with had a rough time. A lot of the German locals were kind, but some of the younger people were very aggressive about so many students working in what they called 'their' factories. It all sounded so different. There's lots of provision made for the unemployed over there. Pity it isn't true here, then Marc would be safe. What it means though is that a lot of heavy work is done by foreigners. Ed was working with Italian and Turkish men. He said he hated not being able to understand what was being said, but equally, he would know by the tone of someone's voice when anger was in the air. And there was a lot of anger. He never wants to go back.

'You would know if you were in a pub or a beer hall that some of the company were staring at you, saying bad stuff. They called us 'The Irish' with a sneer.'

'But you're English,' I said defensively.

'While I was with my friends I was one of them. It didn't make any difference. We were foreign and that was enough. Isn't that terrible? Some of it was justified. There'd been fights after too much drinking and that added to the problem, but there is a real undercurrent of what felt like hatred.'

It's nearly the year 2,000, and yet what Ed was talking about has echoes of long ago. When Ed told me that some of the trouble-makers were as young as fourteen I felt ashamed. At our age we know that we can improve things so much. If they've already started hating, it feels kind of hopeless.

'Don't look so sad, Ness. I'm back, I'm safe and I have money. Lots of lovely money. We are all going out, this weekend, a trip to Fota, as planned.'

We talked about that last year. Fota is a wildlife park. I really want to see it.

'I must ring Tina,' Ed says.

'I thought you had a new girlfriend in Germany.'

'She wasn't really my girlfriend. She was a friendly face who spoke good English and despaired of my German. All I learnt was *spritz*, that means, great. But that's about it.'

How anyone can go away and not pick up any of the language is beyond me. Edward is ringing Tina. He told me that he missed her while he was away. That makes a change. Normally he confuses me with his turnover of girlfriends. I always promise myself I will not get to know them. Then I do. Then he changes his mind and finds someone new. And I end up liking them still and missing them. Definitely not good for Aideen.

Thinking of Aideen, we're trying on our outfits tomorrow. Sorcha, Elly and Aideen are driving over here. I hope we can see what Sorcha is wearing. According to Aideen it's a state secret. Eleanora can't keep a secret, of that I'm sure. But I can't wait to see Ed's reaction when he meets up with her.

'How was Mum in her last letter to you?' He asked.

'Fine. She was talking about joining a writers' group. She wants to start on a book or something when she gets home.'

'A book. How is she meant to write a book, lecture, keep us off the streets and keep Peter at bay?'

I shrugged my shoulders. Then, because even though I like Peter better than I did, I asked the question. 'Do you think Mum will marry him?'

He's all right, but he isn't anything like Dad. I know there isn't a carbon copy of our father wandering around the streets of Cork. It's just that, helpful as Peter can be, he's wrong for her.

I didn't notice Ed creeping over and suddenly grabbing my legs. I was on the floor and he was holding tightly onto my two hands.

'Repeat after me.'

'No.'

'I, Vanessa Carter.'

'I, Vanessa Carter.'

'Am going to stop worrying.'

I said it.

'About things beyond my control.'

'Like you?'

Later, I looked at the letters from Mum, especially the first one, and the card. I haven't shown it to Ed. It feels like it's something between Mum and me. I know I hate secrets, but this is something private, not secretive; there is a difference. I also have never shown Ed a pebble I keep. It was on Dad's grave. Just before we left England, I took it. Mum knows.

What Mum does not know is that about six months ago Ed applied for his driving test. It's in two weeks time. He and Mrs Dineen are going to put in loads of

116

practice. She let Ed drive back from the airport when we went to collect him. There wasn't one angry word, and as long as I kept my eyes shut, he drove beautifully.

'Slow down on the corners,' Mrs D coaxed, and he did. I hope he passes his test. He and Mum can get on each other's nerves, but if Ed can get out for a while, it will make things easier. It must be odd starting off with a squidgy non-talking baby and ending up with a giant loud-mouthed six-footer. This family business is totally confusing. So's *The Great Gatsby*. I've borrowed one of Mum's ten-inch thick tomes to read instead. No, it is not the history of English literature. It's a romance set in the Pacific. Well, even a great brain like mine needs a holiday!

Twenty-seven

Whoever you are, you have to go to Fota. Fota makes you forget weddings, personal disasters, concerns over force-fed calves and errant brothers! Go with lots of friends, take a picnic and extra food, good food, not junk. The reason why you need extra is for the spider monkeys and the lemurs and the slow, shy monkeys who creep warily along trees that look as if they belong in another age. I was prepared to be happy. We were all together. I knew it was going to be a good day. But I was overtaken by cheeky Emus who poked their nosey beaks into our bags. One of them wouldn't leave us alone.

I had spider monkeys with their babies clinging on either side, sitting patiently on my knee waiting to be given a minuscule bit more apple, a trace of orange. Damien had brought peanuts. I was amazed at the delicate fingers of the lemurs as they held the peanuts and quietly chewed, allowing us to watch. There was a brand new cheetah there. It looked like a very handsome kitten, the sort that neither Mrs Carberry nor I will ever come across. It was so perfect. We saw flamingos and listened to peacocks. Everything was exactly how I had imagined it could be. Sometimes things do work out as you plan them.

'You're in heaven. I can tell,' Clara said.

'Isn't it brilliant?' Trass whispered.

We were watching, and listening to some huge apes on an island. They were calling and crying. It sounded exactly like Tarzan.

'*L'amour,*' Ed added.

I gave him a very hard and sisterly stare.

'Isn't it incredible! I've been here dozens of times but every time I'm surprised. They are making mating calls, Ness. Stop looking as if it's a crime. They are literally shouting the loudest.' And Damien suddenly took hold of my hand. Embarrassed, I disappeared into one of the bags with sandwiches. Damien is into touching hands anyway. But all that calling felt like a live biology lesson. It's not that I'm a prude, but it sounded so anguished. I felt dislocated, like a bit of Chris's lego. I was falling apart. Plus my cheeks were going as pink as shrimps. I am convinced my body is a traitor to my mind. The moment I want to seem in control of a situation you could place bets on my nose needing to sneeze or my foot having to be scratched. Worse, the instant I really want to say a very important thing, my words join up and I sound as if I haven't slept for a few years. Ah well!

'Ness, can I have a minute?' Trass, intense, dark, little, interrupted my contemplation. I thought that she'd noticed how uncomfortable I was, but the way she looked made me feel concerned. I suddenly stopped thinking about me. She didn't say anything at first. We walked silently and sat by a pond watching the ducks squabbling over food, diving into the water with their ridiculous tails poking upwards.

'I need to sort something out,' she said, looking into the distance.

She's tiny and she's only just beginning not to have perpetual colds. She makes me feel very protective.

'You are probably the most generous person I know, and I hate doing this to you, again.'

What's she talking about?

'Ness, do you think we could sort out something for me to wear at the wedding? I have shoes, but maybe that skirt you have. Do you mind?'

There I was imagining some high drama. I don't know what. Trass having to move? Her grandfather dying?

'I thought you were going to say something earth shattering,' I laughed. Trass still looked downcast.

'You know how I hate asking.' Oh, Trass. I gave her a giant hug.

'What was that for?'

'Absolutely nothing. I'm practising being demonstrative.'

'Well, don't do it to me too often. You almost broke my ribs!'

By this time the others were strolling back over to us. Aideen was walking beside Ed, listening intently to everything he was saying. I am going to have to talk to her. She looked like an obedient pup. All this being submissive makes me uncomfortable. Aideen has a strong personality. I can accept her liking Ed but I cannot accept her trailing around as if only he exists. It reminds me of Aunt Fran and Uncle Tony. Uncle Tony is a headmaster and whether in or out of school he barks orders to anyone who'll listen; that's only Aunt Fran when they're at our house. I wonder sometimes if my poor aunt has any fight left in her or has it all been washed away.

The last time that they were staying with us I couldn't count the number of times Tony was doing nothing but insisted that Fran took over looking after the children. It's hard to believe that Dad and he were brothers. Dad enjoyed playing games, reading stories, taking us upstairs at bedtime. I suppose families produce all sorts. Come to think of it, where did Ed discover his amazing ability to flirt? Maybe Mum is a reformed man-eater? No. Not possible. But I am definitely going to bring her to Fota. I have so much to tell her. And tonight, when I get the chance, I am going to have a serious chat with Aideen.

Tonight we are going to a disco and tomorrow we are buying school books and having lunch in town. Isn't life brilliant when things go right? All the exciting arrangements that I thought would happen at the beginning of the holidays are now tumbling into place. All but one; in my happy state I almost forgot the wedding.

Twenty-eight

'Did you find the spare mattresses, Ness?' Mrs Dineen, calling from the bottom of the stairs, wants to know.

'Yeah. It's okay. I have all the beds made up.'

Clara, Aideen and Trass are staying the night and we're getting ready to go to a disco. My room looks like a transit camp. There are sleeping bags and pillows piled in heaps in amongst clothes, shoes, cassettes and the cats.

'Does it still house the local flea population?' Clara asks, pointing in the direction of my most uncomplicated of companions, Puss.

'No.' Clara is not an animal person. As she said, she respects their space as long as they respect her's. Right now Puss is definitely invading her portion of the room. He is cuddling into the T-shirt that she's thrown off, and kneading it ecstatically.

'What do you think?' Trass is pirouetting in a peach and cream flared skirt that Mum found in Dublin last year. I ask you, peach and cream, for me? The poor woman is so full of good intentions. Please God don't let her have bought clothes for me in America. I will hate them. I will pretend to be happy about them – otherwise she gets hurt – then I will hide them away, until they are too small, like the skirt.

'Is the top too big?'

Trass is looking anxiously at herself in my full length mirror. I had stuck a load of cut-outs from magazines over the mirror. Waking up to the whole picture of me was not an inspiration, but in my absence, Mrs D has removed them, pasted them onto a board and left the mirror ready for another laughing session.

'Trass, it is not too big,' I reassure her. What I was tempted to say was that if it were any tighter she would be inviting the vice squad back for coffee. Trass, like me, sees her version of herself and needs constant reassurance that it's only half as bad as she thinks it is.

'Have Trass and Clara seen the bridesmaids' concoctions yet?' Aideen wants to know.

That girl spends her life doing her teeth. She's obsessed. Tonight she is leaving out the brace. I'm lucky, I suppose. I've never had to wear one. The dentist probably looked at my tombstone teeth and decided I was beyond help. I keep wondering if it's my reflection or the glass that makes them look yellow. Who cares, we're going to the disco and then back here for videos. Mrs Dineen is staying the night as well.

'I'll be waiting with something for you all to eat. You'll probably be ravenous.'

What she is doing is making sure that we get back safely, but unlike those who fuss she puts it in such a way as not to offend. How did she learn to do that? Maybe the combination of once being a teacher and a mum? No, that can't be it; Mum wears exactly the same two hats and she has the most incredible ability to say the wrong thing. If she were here right now she'd be fussing over the fact that I'm wearing cut-off denim shorts. I would be arguing that it's hot tonight. She would say, 'Wear a skirt.' I would begin by explaining why what I'm wearing was right. She would initially, patiently, give me her reason why I'm wrong. I would flounce off. Ed would mediate and we'd go out knowing that she was at home, miserable and lonely, or worse, miserable and ringing Peter to come over and keep her company. She tries.

'Well, have you shown Clara and Trass the ...' Lost for words, Aideen is waving her hands around herself trying to describe our Eleanora Stratton originals.

'Can't we surprise them on the day?'

'That bad,' says Clara sympathetically.

Aideen gives me a knowing look, and Trass and Clara shake their heads together in commiseration. Ah well! Tonight we don't have to worry about all of that. My only concern is that Tina isn't coming with us, so my promised chat with Aideen will have to wait. Ed seemed disappointed, even a bit upset. That will be a new experience for him, rejection. No, that's cruel. I don't want anyone hurt.

'Ness, where's the gloss?' Aideen is digging around amongst the boxes that I collect. I like little boxes, but they are beginning to make my dressing table look like a packing factory. Finding it I suddenly notice Clara. Where did big, jolly Clara disappear to? She is tall all right, and she is still jolly, but decked out in lycra shorts and a baggy shirt she looks like one of those girls you envy in teen magazines. Maybe I should wear something else.

'There's no rush back. I have a book that I can't put down to read. I have the late night film, and I'll be looking forward to hearing about how you all get on.' Mrs D is opening the door and almost pushing us out into the bright evening light.

It stays light much longer here in Cork than it did in Colchester. Ed agrees, the others think I'm joking. Maybe because there is less pollution. But it's great being able to walk along at nine-thirty and everything is still sunny. It's as if the rain of the last decade has been forgotten. Reinforce yourself, disco floor. Vanessa

Carthorse is on her way!

I am not a natural dancer, I promise you. I am trying to sway to the music but the lights are hurting my eyes. If I shut them, I fall to one side, which might look like an original new step, but it means I crash into the others.

The floor is heaving. There are bodies gyrating. It's like some wild tribal dance. I'm out there on the floor with Damien. It's wonderful to be dancing with him. Over in the far corner I see Ed, talking to Aideen. I don't know how they can hear what they're saying. This is Bedlam; worse, it's deafening. This is really not such a bad experience at all.

Twenty-nine

'And what may I ask are those?' Mrs Carberry wants to know. She's perched as usual on her sofa bed, with Pru the Persian cat elegantly draped on her slippered feet. And the Yorkie is scratching at the back door asking to be let out.

'It's a miracle. The dog asked to be let out,' I announce letting the yapping, silky-haired creation into the backyard which Cassie now sweeps on a daily basis. I just hope that her right hook isn't improving with all this exercise. She's a dangerous enough fighter as it is.

'Did you hear me?' Mrs Carberry is an impatient old lady. She's looking much better though. The shower is now installed. So far she doesn't need any help. I will dread it when she does, but Jo keeps reassuring me that she or Mrs Mac will be there. That doesn't make me feel any easier, but seeing as I've promised to start action aid on my doorstep I can't drop out now.

'Well!' Mrs Carberry is so like Cassie. As soon as Cassie sees a parcel she assumes that it's for her. Mrs C is exactly the same.

'School books. I've just been to buy next year's books.' They cost a fortune, and that was after I'd queued for an hour and bought some second hand. In England they were there, waiting in a cupboard. Here I own them. Do I really want to own all these maths books, these German and Italian texts? Oh but they look boring! The queuing bit was crazy. We'd sorted out our lists but it didn't make any difference. For some unknown reason I ended up with a whole load of art equipment and I don't even do art! Take it from me, it was a mess. The girl at the counter was very patient, considering how giggly we suddenly became.

Lunch in the park was a success; cheesy croissants are a great invention! The discovery that we had totally forgotten Ed's books only made us laugh more. He should have been with us, but right now he's in the middle of taking his driving test. Please let him pass. Damien and Toby have disappeared to the Phelans, Trass's neighbours. There's been some more trouble. Paudie Phelan has a large dog who tends to wander the streets and has recently taken to stealing people's milk cartons left outside the door. He's not a bad dog, but that's not how other folk see it. So a big fence is being erected to keep him in. I hope it works. Anyway, it was an interesting morning.

'Show me, then.'

I give the bag to Mrs Carberry and begin to wash a few dishes. There is the remains of a little casserole; that was from Trass's Mum. Quite often, not every day, she brings down small meals. If we overdo things Mrs Carberry sulks for hours. But remembering Peter's warning of no scraps for the pets, I ditch the leftovers.

'Ah. *Tender is the Night*. Scotty. Poor man.' Mrs Carberry, nose almost into the page. She's lost her glasses yet again.

'Scotty. Is he a missing canine or what?' I ask.

'Don't be cheeky. Tell young Cass that I want her to find a photograph album.'

Mrs C can suddenly become enormously energetic. Now is one of those moments. Giving Pru a poke the regal creature sidles off, making towards upstairs.

'No, you don't.' Picking him up I push him outside

127

the front door. We've blocked off upstairs. The roof is halfway mended but the rain keeps pouring and the slates keep falling. All the furniture is covered with fresh sheets and the wallpaper is gradually falling off with the aid of kitchen knives and the weather. It was so odd. At first we wanted to make the place safe, nothing more. Then Mrs Carberry gave her bank book to Mrs McDermot. I was so thrilled. Lots of local people wouldn't give Trass's Mum the plastic off their tray of meat. But Mrs Carberry told her that it would be good to have some repairs done, and that she'd accumulated a bit of money over the years. I don't know how much, that's between Trass's Mum and Jo. They are sorting finances, but we've worked wonders on the old place.

The hall is opened out and painted. The front door has a lock; the back door is secure. Luckily she doesn't keep money stuffed in mattresses, nor does she have to do her shopping any more! She has a little fridge, and now I can drink milk without feeling sick at the thought of a warm glass. Things are improving.

'Cassandra,' Mrs Carberry calls impatiently.

'I couldn't find it at first,' Cass replies handing Mrs Carberry an ornate photograph album.

'Where did you find that?' I want to know. Cassie's answer is a full mouth of sweets and a rather vulgar float of her fingers in the air.

'Now, here's Scotty.'

Looking at the picture, all brown and spotted with age, I can see Scott Fitzgerald, the writer. Sitting next to him, a very young Dorothy Barton with a wide-brimmed glass in her hand. It doesn't seem real, even though it's true that the young woman chatting in the sunshine all those years ago is the old cantankerous lady sitting opposite me right now.

'He wanted us for *The Beautiful and the Damned*. But we were more than happy taking the plays of writers like Synge abroad,' Mrs Carberry is musing.

Cassie keeps turning pages. I recognise Orson Welles, Gary Cooper, James Stewart, old actors who were once famous and whom you can still see on Sunday afternoons in black and white films. If I wait, surely now she will say something about her past.

'Put it back where you found it, Cass,' Mrs Carberry asks. Obediently Cassie gets up and disappears into the hall and presumably upstairs. Nobody on this earth can make Cassie do something instantly, apart from Mrs C.

'Nothing surprises you, does it, Miss Knowledgeable Ness?' she suddenly says, fussing with her cardigan buttons.

'Everything surprises me.'

'Good.'

'But I do know.' I need to say it.

'Of course you do. But you haven't made me a charity case. Marie and Jo, the lad with the fringe (Marc) and his friends, they've added a real sparkle to my life. You're a good girl, Vanessa, and keep on enunciating those words. I've noticed recently that you're slurring them'.

Oh, Mrs Carberry. Is that it? There's masses we could talk about. I would love to know about Scott Fitzgerald, the writer of one of my set books, *The Great Gatsby*. I know you can't have all that much time left, but I can't push you. I want to but I daren't. This friendship thing is very fragile. I don't want to break the spell. What will my mother make of you? If she tries to muscle-in I'll ... Now I sound like Cass.

Thirty

Ed and I are in the kitchen. We cleaned windows yesterday. I wish the sun would shine in a different direction because, at the moment, all this bright light is showing up dirty big streak marks. Going back to school will be a relief after all this housework. You would have thought that some inventor could have come up with self-wash surfaces by now.

'What time did you say she's arriving?' Ed wants to know. He's wearing Mum's Garfield apron and the globs of pastry dripping from his fingers make him look like a productive, if not a professional, chef.

'Seven forty-five, a quarter to eight. In six hours!' I have checked the date (August the twentieth) so often on the calendar that it now looks as if a truck-load of field mice have gone hiking over the page.

Two days ago unexpected things suddenly started happening. Mrs Dineen has had to disappear to Ballycotton in a hurry; her mother had a fall and needs looking after. We reassured Mrs D that everything was well under control, which it was until I had the brilliant idea that we should cook a cordon bleu meal as a welcome home treat for Mum. It isn't that cooking is difficult, but I think we might be trying to be a bit ambitious with what we've chosen to cook. And how do you time everything so that it all ends up ready at the same moment? Preparing in advance felt like a good move when we woke up, but we seem to have been scraping, podding, mixing and mashing all day.

Clara and her parents are coming over for a drink

this evening. I was pleased about Clara and a bit less sure about Mr and Mrs Farrell. They tend to be rather proper. Peter will be here too. It's going to be strange having the house packed with adults again. Unfortunately some of our major plans haven't quite materialised; the biggest being that Ed would pick up Mum, because Ed should have passed his driving test. He didn't. The dumb examiner failed him for driving too slowly and approaching a junction with undue caution! Peter is collecting Mum from the airport.

'I can drive. I know the rules. I'm safe,' Ed kept saying. I agree but Mum would collapse on the spot were he to arrive without an official piece of paper slapped on his forehead for everyone to see, pronouncing him fully licensed. Poor Ed.

Doubly poor Ed. Tina has a new boyfriend. I think my brother is truly hurt. Aideen is delighted and listens to him going on for hours about how right he and Tina were for each other, how for the first time in his life he was really involved and so on. Aideen nods away like some recently hatched agony aunt. I have a low boredom threshold, plus I've heard it all before. But there is a very-much-together couple padding around the place, Emma and Puss. Where he hops she follows. He's on permanent parade with his little companion like a silvery shadow beside him. Do cats show off? Mine seem to. I know that things have been a bit sloppier without Mum around but Puss is carrying things too far. He used to have a vague idea of accepted cat territory. Now they can both be found sleeping in the tumble drier, claw sharpening on the back door and eating anything that's left on whatever surface is available.

Tonight is beginning to feel like a tricky prospect. I

don't think Peter's bill is going to make my mother love me to death either. Rescuing strays is proving expensive. Mum will probably have to re-mortgage the house. What would create a nice atmosphere? I know.

'Why don't we light a fire in the sitting room. It's getting cold at night and if we bought a load of candles, pulled the curtains, piled on the old logs ...'

I can see it already. It always looks lovely that way. Not that we go into the sitting room much but it does have a Christmassy feel once it's dark outside and there's sprinkly light inside. Mum had all the chairs re-covered and stuck down a pale carpet. As soon as I see anything pale that's meant to be treated with care, I either spill blackcurrant juice all over the place, or drop my marmite sandwiches in a fit of nerves and then proceed to tread on them. Absolutely no blackcurrant and emphatically no marmite. I preferred the room before it was smartened up but Mum decided she needed somewhere decent for entertaining. Well, tonight is an entertaining kind of night.

Twenty minutes to go and Ed's beef smells revolting; it must be cooking by now. In our enthusiasm we forgot the timer was set on the oven, so when we thought we'd turned it on, we hadn't. I miss you, Mrs D. There we were, traipsing around craft shops spending a fortune on carved candles and Ed's culinary delicacy was sitting getting very cold in the unheated stove. Everywhere looks fine. The new potatoes have parsley shredded all over them, the salad is glistening with a bit too much olive oil, but it's good for our hearts, I hope. I have temporarily resolved the pet dilemma by giving them a large mohair jumper to sleep on. They are snuggled in the airing cupboard. Please let it all go well.

Thirty-one

It's getting light outside. We didn't need the fire-brigade, luckily. But Ed and I will be without money for the next hundred years. Maybe running away to sea wouldn't be such a bad idea after all. There have to be equal opportunities on board some ships. Looking back on it, bits of our 'welcome home' party could have been a success. Mum said how much she enjoyed rare beef and Peter had already warned her about the kitten. She was even quite calm about my using her jumper. It didn't look that new to me with all those shaggy bits hanging off it and it's angora, not mohair. Whatever, Emma is very attached to it.

'Why don't we go into the other room?' Ed suggested after the meal and just as the Farrells arrived. After all, it was our big treat, the fire, the candles.

'Won't it be a bit damp and cold in there?' Mum wanted to know. She was all kindness and consideration and glowing with happiness to be back and to see us both safe and well. We should have recorded that moment.

The next bit feels as if it was in slow motion but it must have happened quite quickly. I saw Clara's dad walking ahead of Mum down the hall and going towards the door to push it open. Mum was carrying a tray of drinks and Peter was collecting something from the car. Clara and Ed were clearing up in the kitchen and then we heard a crash — that was the tray falling. The roar that followed the crash could have been measured on the Richter scale.

'Edward! Vanessa!'

We looked at each other and ran.

There really wasn't too much that we could say. Everything was not romantic. It was black! In the candlelight it looked a bit like a spooky stage-set. It didn't seem like the real thing. It was.

'You're lucky you didn't lose the chimney,' Mr Farrell was saying as he tripped over furniture looking for lights.

'All your lovely things,' muttered Mrs Farrell, lovingly stroking the sooty cabinet housing the sooty crystal.

'What? How?' Ed kept spluttering odd words and questions. I stood there and for some unknown reason couldn't get it out of my head that something like this had happened before, a very long time ago. Then was not the right time to start enquiring about other past disasters.

What had happened this time round was that our lovely fire had done exactly what a fire is meant to do. We'd used paper and peat briquettes and left it burning away with a few logs on top. That would have been around six o'clock. I lit candles only seconds before Mum arrived and checked that everything was looking good. Obviously our fire got bored chewing away at all the conventional stuff and took off along a most unsuspected route. Old soot that had been stacking up nicely since we arrived at the house became heated and dropped down onto the logs, into the hearth ... Now this bit was lucky; eventually the flames were put out. But more and more soot had become dislodged and had fallen. If you drop a bag of flour it sprays out white powder that covers everything in sight. I know, I've done it, not intentionally, but it spreads. Soot does the same, only it is very black. It smells bad and it creeps and stains.

According to Mum we are going to have to get professional cleaners in to deal with most of the mess. That's where Ed and I are involved. We are going to have to pay for them. I remember way back, before the end of term, that Mum mentioned getting chimneys swept as part of what had to be done during the holidays. Come to think of it, there was a note somewhere. But it didn't happen.

The cats are locked in the garage. I can't blame Mum for being angry and she isn't so much angry as devastated. It was her best room. That's the trouble with 'best' things. But I didn't see why Puss and Emma had to be punished for something that was a total accident. Ed recovered sufficiently to stop me from getting involved in a massive argument.

'She's tired, Ness. She'll see it differently tomorrow. It's not a cold night. Those two animals have their fur and each other to keep them warm,' he advised me as we were closing the front door.

I don't want to think about tomorrow. And what about the wedding? Welcome back, Mum.

Ed is depressed. The prospect of one more year at school, no car, no girlfriend and no money have left him pretty miserable.

'The presents were good.' I keep trying to say something soothing and helpful. Mum bought us each a portable CD player, headphones, the lot. It's just as well that she gave them to us when she was chewing her way through dinner on the first night home. Otherwise I think she might have done something rather more fatal with her gifts.

'Great! Even better if I could afford to buy CDs.'

'True enough.' I seem to be doing a lot of sighing lately.

Mum has been back for three days. In the past I sometimes objected to Mrs Dineen's being around when things were a bit awkward here. Now I can't wait to see her. She rang, the morning after Mum returned. It was a short conversation, enough to let us know her mother is recovering and to find out about Mum's American adventure. When I heard the word 'soot' I scattered outside rapidly. There are some four-letter words that ought to be struck from the dictionary. Soot is one of them.

I must go and see Mrs Carberry later. The last visit was on the way to the dry cleaners with the curtains. Ed was with me. In fact he hasn't been far away for the last few days. I don't think that he knows how to make it up to Mum. Neither do I. Anyway, Mrs Carberry made us tea and listened to what had happened. She laughed.

'It isn't funny,' I said.

'No, it's a pity for you both but it's a bigger pity for your mother. When am I going to meet her?' I didn't like to say never. As Mum and I are only conversing around the bare essentials I haven't gone into too much detail about what we've been doing all summer.

Thirty-two

It's Wednesday. Aideen and I are in the front pew of St Peter's church and I think I'm going to faint. Seeing as I have never in my life fainted, now would be extremely inconvenient. Normally Wednesday is nicely placed in the centre of the week. Today it is the centre of my universe; for ever more it will be re-named wedding day. We have finally reached a sitting-down part of the ceremony. I'm sure that Sorcha's dad has needed to sit throughout the whole thing. I only hope that he took out a big enough loan to pay for all these people. They've come in coach-loads!

This morning was crazy. Mum had me out of bed by seven, over to Aideen's at nine. I must not fall asleep but the smell of flowers and the droning of voices is making me dozy. One thing is for sure, I am changing into something different the very second I get out of here.

'Oh Nessie,' Mum said when she saw me in my bridesmaid's thing, 'you look so lovely.'

Lovely I am not but it's not bad considering it's a skirt; apparently the material is called tulle. I thought it was a pair of net curtains at first. And the scoopy tops would be fine if Elly had remembered that both Aideen and I appear to have been doing chest expanding exercises over the last few months. We haven't, but that's what it looks like. I'm in purple, Aideen in mauve. It could be worse, not much, but at least we didn't trip up on the way down behind Sorcha and her Dad.

This is it. The organ is playing so loudly the plaster could fall off the ceiling at any minute. Sorcha is smiling wildly at us and even Rory is giving us a grin. Cassie has appeared at my side. I could hear her yelling at me from the back of the church.

'Can I have your flowers?' she wants to know.

'Yes, as long as you don't eat them or do something awful to Chris with them.' She probably will. I never thought that I would consider missing a four-year-old but then Cassie is different.

I had a chance to talk to Sorcha this morning while Aideen was having a bath and Mrs O'Hare was flapping around downstairs organising uncles, aunts, grannies and long-lost relatives from all over the world. They make a big deal out of weddings in this country! Anyway, sitting in Sorcha's bedroom, surrounded by posters and old school books and all the dolls that she's collected from every imaginable foreign country I had to say it.

'Are you sure you're truly happy about all this?'

She looked amazing. Elly is a big disappointment. Sorcha's dress is perfect, in fact, it's almost identical to the shape of the dress that Mrs C wore at her wedding. It isn't a crinoline, more like a tulip. I like it.

'I was wondering when you were going to ask something outrageous.' It didn't feel outrageous.

'Do you know why I haven't asked you, or Aideen or Mum or Dad come to think of it, what they think of Rory? I don't want to know. It's not that I'm afraid of other people's opinions but, quite simply, I am happy with the way I feel.' I didn't mean it, but occasionally I do a snarly face without intending.

'He's a very special man, Ness.'

He is?

'I knew it almost immediately. I'm a lot better nurse and midwife than I am an air hostess. I know that I pour a good gin and tonic, and yes, the travelling has been fun, but it was always temporary. When I got to know Rory, and when he told me about San Christos, that was it.'

You can say that again.

'He's a good doctor and he's a magic person. I love him, Ness.'

And that was it. What more could I say. But I did want to hear her say it, the 'I love him' bit. Come to think of it they look remarkably like each other. Aideen told me the other day that Sorcha dyes her eye-lashes. God help their kids. I'd better start saving for a do-it-yourself family lash kit.

Aideen is having a quick sniffle. Just as well Mum has tissues. She gave us the first batch during the ring exchanging part. I wasn't crying but I felt a touch emotional. Weddings are a bit awesome. My bright plan to wear waterproof mascara has probably saved Aideen's day. There's nothing quite so horrible as a streaky face after a good old sob. We are almost at the door of the church now. I feel as if I've walked the length and breadth of a football pitch. Now let's get on with the party bit, the reception. But not before I change into something comfortable. All things considered it wasn't nearly as bad as I thought it was going to be.

What a strange day! I suppose that 'big' days like weddings and communions and confirmations have to be, otherwise they'd get lost in amongst any other old Wednesday or Thursday. I wouldn't choose to go through it all again but it was a lot better than I was expecting. I'm a bit annoyed though. I spent all summer dreading what turned out to be in some ways amazing! As usual I have insomnia. That will mean more ulcers on my tongue. They hurt. Mum called in a second ago to check that I was okay. She's going to allow Ed to drive the car. He's over the moon. She let him drive her home this evening and was full of compliments; there wasn't so much as a dark look. I think the wine and the champagne helped, but Ed was thrilled with all the praise.

My cats are missing. I'm leaning out of the window trying to call quietly. Everything sounds as if I've turned up the volume and added a few extra speakers for effect. Why don't they go hunting during daylight hours? I worry about drivers who don't worry about missing moggies. I have a sneaking suspicion that some people even make a sport out of cat bashing. As opposed to that, if my personal killer squad reappear tomorrow and leave bits of some poor dead creature on the doorstep, I will absolutely refuse to clear it up. Being an animal owner is not an easy choice. Being a tired and concerned animal owner is exhausting.

Ed and I had a long chat at the reception. Special food had been organised for me and several of Rory's friends. They were from India and not only do they not eat meat, they don't drink milk or have any dairy produce either. I'm not that dedicated but they were interesting. Anyway, while I was picking through saffron rice and trying to dislodge nuts from my teeth Ed suddenly announced that he's giving up women for a year. I don't believe him. But he had the desired effect. I almost choked; most unbecoming.

Ed has organised to see a counsellor. This person advises students about courses at college and job prospects and so on. He really does seem determined.

Elly joined us. She was such a failure as young, expressive designer of the year. My mother looked more bizarre than she did. I told Elly.

'You don't look the same with hair and a dress and a shoulder bag. You realise that you're copping out,' I said.

'Just for today, Ness. I don't think Sorcha or Rory would be too happy with some of the stuff that I have on my drawing board at the moment. As opposed to that ...' She has invited Aideen and me to go to Dublin, any time, to have a look at her new ideas. We might. I have a lot of free weekends ahead of me what with Damien disappearing and Jo and Marc. I don't want to think about it. Marc has been offered a job in Holland. He has no choice. I am stunned, but for the first time in my non-relationship with Damien *I* did the comforting. The Kellehers leaving is going to change everything. What am I going to do without them? What am I going to do without Damien?

Thirty-three

'It is a new school year, a new term. For some of you it's your first year at City Community. Welcome.'

The headmaster must have spent the summer in an igloo; he's paler now than he was in June. One of those new pupils is Ophelia Kelleher. She's about twelve rows ahead of us, in ordinary clothes because as Jo said, there wasn't much point in buying a uniform, just in case. For 'just in case' I understand that this job of Marc's might last a lot longer than I want to think about. But, for the next two weeks things are as normal as they can be (Damien, Toby, Ophelia, Sophie, Hugh and Darragh will still go to school.) Not that big assembly like this is normal. There must be around six hundred of us packed into the main hall for the head's opening address. I missed out on the experience last year. I think that I would have run away instantly had I been confronted by this gathering. Damien has had his hair cut. Where his pony tail used to be is a very white neck.

'And we have two fresh groups of examinees, for third and sixth years. All your efforts are to be tested and your futures made a little more certain.'

Why would he say something like that? About the only certain bit of future I can foresee is a lot of work and plenty of headaches. It's good having Mrs Dineen back at home. She's the only person in the house who knows where Mum hides the aspirin! Mrs D's mum is staying with her for now. She must be some tough old lady; despite all the drama and being given the last rites and everything she's pottering around and according to Mrs D insists on watching television from the moment she wakes up until she goes to bed. I will definitely have to introduce her to Mrs Carberry. They can watch the horse racing together. I still find it confusing that somebody as old as ninety-four has a heart that is perkily ticking away. In my muddled head I can't find one good reason why Dad isn't here enjoying this place the same as we are. But then we wouldn't have come here if he were still around.

Walking back down the long corridor with all the familiar statues polished and in place, I'm wondering where my lovely three months went to. It's as if we've never been away. As usual I feel hungry. I only have to see our classroom and instantly I feel ravenous. I suppose it's knowing that I can't eat until first break that does it. Clara has saved me a seat and Enda is patting the chair beside her for Damien to sit down. Catherine is sharpening a pencil, looking bored. Everything is the same. Did the holidays happen? Was it all a dream?

The English teacher has given us an essay for this evening, 'My Summer Plans'. Inspirational. She probably took all the holidays thinking up that boring title. I read some of Mum's book last night. It's creepy reading something by someone you know. It isn't as I imagined a book she'd write would be. For a start it's a travel story. She hasn't decided what to call it yet, but it has to be better than any planning done during the summer! I can't think of anything except Fota that worked out as I imagined it might. And looking after Hugh's turtles from here to whenever is another surprise. All I can think of is what we didn't do. But we made a quilt, which we've given to Mrs C. The wedding came and went and Sorcha sent a postcard from somewhere unpronounceable and sounded fine. My rabbit is still without ears, and I haven't yet swum in a lake or a river. Yes, the holidays happened and they're over.

Aideen will visit at the weekend. There's going to be a farewell party for the Kellehers. If I shut my eyes I can still imagine what it felt like dancing with Damien, sitting at the table with him, being pushed out of his room for being a pain.

'Would you like to share the joke with us, Vanessa?' the English teacher is asking.

Here we go. I am smiling and so are most of the class. Third year has very definitely begun. 'Miss, about that essay title ...'